BLUE CHRISTMAS

BOOKS BY MARY KAY ANDREWS

Bright Lights, Big Christmas
The Homewreckers
The Santa Suit
The Newcomer
Hello, Summer
Sunset Beach
The High Tide Club
The Weekenders
Beach Town
Save the Date
Christmas Bliss
Ladies' Night
Spring Fever
Summer Rental
The Fixer Upper
Deep Dish
Savannah Breeze
Blue Christmas
Hissy Fit
Little Bitty Lies
Savannah Blues

PREVIOUSLY PUBLISHED UNDER THE
NAME KATHY HOGAN TROCHECK

Irish Eyes
Midnight Clear
Crash Course
Strange Brew
Lickety Split
Heart Trouble
Happy Never After
Homemade Sin
To Live and Die in Dixie
Every Crooked Nanny

NONFICTION
The Beach House Cookbook

BLUE CHRISTMAS

Mary Kay Andrews

HARPER

NEW YORK ● LONDON ● TORONTO ● SYDNEY

HARPER

A hardcover edition of this book was published in 2006 by HarperCollins Publishers.

HarperCollins books may be purchased for educational, business, or sales promotional use. For information, please email the Special Markets Department at SPsales@harpercollins.com.

FIRST HARPER PAPERBACKS EDITION PUBLISHED 2012; REISSUED 2019, 2023.

Designed by Joy O'Meara
Ornaments by Kara Strubel

The Library of Congress has catalogued the hardcover edition as follows:

Andrews, Mary Kay.
  Blue Christmas / Mary Kay Andrews.—1st ed.
    p. cm.
  ISBN 978-0-06-083734-1
  1. Savannah (Ga)—Fiction. 2. Christmas—Fiction. I. Title.
  PS3570.R587B58 2006
813'.6—dc22   2006041087

ISBN 978-0-06-295397-1 (pbk.)
23 24 25 26 27 LBC 9 8 7 6 5

*For my Savannah posse: Polly Powers Stramm and
Jacky Blatner Yglesias, with love and thanks
for all the years of friendship and fun*

CHAPTER 1

I was just hot-gluing the last popcorn-and-cranberry strand to the second of two five-foot-high topiary Christmas trees when my best friend came breezing into Maisie's Daisy.

BeBe Loudermilk stopped dead in her tracks and gazed around the first floor of my antiques shop, wrinkling her nose in distaste.

She gestured toward the half-empty crates of apples, oranges, and kumquats scattered around my worktable, at the halved pineapples and the pomegranates spilling out of grocery sacks, and at the freshly fallen drifts of popcorn littering the floor.

"What the hell?" she said dramatically. There are very few statements BeBe makes that are not laden with drama.

"Are you now turning to fruit vending as a sideline?" She shook her head sadly. "And I thought you were doing so well with the antiques."

"Christmas decorations," I said, pressing the popcorn strings onto the surface of the topiary tree, which I'd already covered with what seemed like a whole orchard full of tiny green crab apples and kumquats. "For the historic district decorating contest."

"Ohhh," she said, drawing it out.

With one tentative fingertip, she tapped the tree I'd completed, knocking off a kumquat, which rolled onto the floor, joining half a dozen other pieces of fallen fruit.

"Cute," she said dismissively.

"Cute? Is that all you can say? Cute? I've spent three whole days with this project. I've blown a good three hundred dollars on fresh fruit and nuts and Styrofoam forms, and strung what feels like ten miles of popcorn and cranberries. And just look at my hands!"

I held them out for her to see. There were needle pricks on my fingertips, hot-glue burns on my palms, and multiple bandages from self-inflicted skewerings.

"Criminal," BeBe said. "But why?"

"Because," I said, "I am, by God, going to win the commercial division decorating contest this year, even if I have to cover the entire surface of this building with every piece of fresh fruit in Savannah."

"Again . . . why would you bother? I mean, what's in it for you?"

"Pride," I said. "Last year I really thought I had it sewn up. Remember, I did that whole deal with the gilded palmetto fronds and magnolia leaf swags? And I had all the dried okra pods and pinecones? And I didn't even make honorable mention? They gave first place to that stupid boutique on Whitaker. Can you believe they won with those lame-o kudzu vines and hokey bird's nests and stuffed cardinals? I mean, stuffed birds! It was absolutely Hitchcockian!"

"A tragic oversight, I'm sure," BeBe said, looking around the shop. "Remind me again why it was so crucial that I come over here today?"

"You promised to watch the shop," I said. "There's an auction at Trader Bob's, over in Hardeeville, that starts at noon. This close to Christmas, I can't afford to close up while I go on a buying trip. I was also hoping you might help me put up all the decorations before I leave in an hour."

She sighed. "All right. What are we doing?"

I gestured toward the pair of topiary trees. "Help me drag these outside. They're going in those big cast-iron urns by the front doors. Then we've got to tack up the over-door plaque with the pineapples and lemons and limes, and swag the grapevines around the show windows. I've got two kinds of grapes—green and red, and we'll hot-glue those once the vines are in place. Then the only thing left is the window display. But I'll set that up once I get back from Hardeeville."

With a maximum amount of huffing and puffing, and some very un-Christmas-like swearing when BeBe broke an acrylic nail, we managed to get the decorations in place.

"There," I said, standing out on the sidewalk, gazing at our masterpiece. "Take that, Babalu!"

"Babalu who?"

"Babalu them," I said, pointing across Troup Square.

"My nearest and queerest competition."

"That's not very nice," she said. "I thought you loved gay men."

"You don't know Manny and Cookie," I told her.

Manny Alvarez and Cookie Parker had opened their shop on Harris Street the previous spring. Manny was a retired landscape designer from Delray Beach, Florida, and Cookie? Well, Cookie *claimed* he'd been a Broadway chorus boy in the road show of *Les Misérables*, but he was fifty if he was a day, going bald, and weighed close to three hundred pounds.

"I tried to be nice and welcoming. I took flowers over there on their opening day, invited them to dinner, but since the minute they opened, they've been trying to put me out of business," I told BeBe. "They've tried to snake some of my best pickers. They called up the city and complained about my customers parking in loading zones; they even went to the gift mart and came back with the exact same line of aromatherapy candles and bath salts I carry, and now they sell them for two bucks cheaper."

"The nerve!" BeBe said. She craned her neck to look across the square at their shop. "Looks like they're working on their Christmas decorations too. Must be half a dozen men swarming around over there. Wow, look. They've got like a phone company truck with one of those cherry-picker buckets hanging lights along the front of the building."

"I'm sure whatever they do will be gaudy as hell," I said, flouncing back into the shop with BeBe following close behind. "Remember what they did for Halloween? The whole façade of the building was a red devil, with the shop's windows lit up with yellow lights as the devil's eyes."

"Hmm," BeBe said noncommittally.

"They blinked off and on all night. I thought I was having a seizure the first time I looked over there and saw it. It damn near drove me nuts," I said. "And it was *so* over the top."

"Not Savannah at all," BeBe agreed. "But flashy. You gotta give 'em that."

"Anybody could do what they've done," I said. "If money was no object. And those two are apparently rolling in it. I heard Manny personally donated twenty thousand dollars for the downtown business district's new Christmas lights. Of course, it's nothing but a thinly veiled attempt to buy the decorating contest."

"That is a lot of cash though," BeBe said. "Where do they get their money?"

"The old-fashioned way," I said. "Inherited. I heard Manny had a much older lover down in Florida who died two years ago. He had a start-up telecommunications company, and when he died, Manny got everything."

"Except good taste," BeBe said. I shot her a grateful look. She really is the world's best best friend.

"All righty then," I said, wiping my hands on the seat of my jeans. "I'm gonna head over to Hardeeville. I should be back by about four. There's plenty of change in the cash register. Prices are marked on everything. Anything brown or orange should be considered Thanksgiving merchandise, and you can mark it down fifty percent. And if you see Manny or Cookie lurking around outside, trying to steal my decorating ideas, just sic Jethro on 'em."

"Jethro?" She sighed heavily.

At the sound of his name, Jethro the shop dog poked his nose out from under the worktable where he'd been hiding, hoping I'd perhaps drop a sausage biscuit along with all that runaway fruit.

"He adores you," I told BeBe. "And he's great company."

"He sheds," BeBe said. "He drools. He farts."

"At least he's consistent," I said, heading out the back door to my pickup truck.

CHAPTER 2

It was one of those winter mornings that remind you why you live in the south. Sunny, with a hint of coolness in the air. Despite the fact that we were less than two weeks away from Christmas, the thick grass in Troup Square was still emerald green, and Spanish moss dripped like old lace from the oaks surrounding the iron armillary in the middle of the square. And on this beautiful winter morning, I was just as thankful for what wasn't as I was for what was: no gnats, no blistering heat, no suffocating humidity.

I should have been headed in the opposite direction, but instead I turned my beat-up old turquoise truck around the square. Just a quick drive by Babalu, I promised myself. Just to reassure myself of how superior my decorations were. But my heart sank as I slowed my roll.

The three-story shrimp pink exterior of Babalu had been transformed. Twining vines magically covered the façade. A pair of towering palm trees in rococo concrete urns flanked the shop's front door, which itself was wreathed in a fabulously elaborate swag of moss, boxwood, smilax, and cedar. Every-thing, including the palm trees, had been painted flat white, then sprinkled with glitter. Hundreds of cut-glass chandelier prisms dangled from the white vines, and sent crystal refrac-tions of light onto the sidewalk. It was a winter wonderland.

And standing right there on the sidewalk, directing the man in the bucket of the cherry picker, was the Snow Queen himself, Manny Alvarez.

"No, darling," he called, cupping his hands to be heard. "You've got the lights all bunched up there on the right side."

The bucket-truck had traffic blocked in front of the shop, and I had no choice but to stop behind it. My truck's brakes made a grinding noise, and Manny whirled around to see where the noise was coming from. A smile lit his face when he spotted me.

"Eloise?" he said, one eyebrow lifted. "Checking on the competition, are we?"

I gritted my teeth. "Hello, Manny. Looks like your side of the square has had some unusual weather for Savannah."

"You know me," he said airily. "Fantasy is my life. And really, that whole nuts and fruits and berries thing all the locals down here seem to be clinging to is so five minutes ago. Don't you agree?"

"The historic commission's guidelines specifically call for using natural, vernacular design elements," I pointed out. "I guess that's why the 'locals' as you call them tend to follow the guidelines."

"Oh, guidelines," he said, shaking his head. "Boring! Cookie and I believe in following our muse, in order to allow the full range of creative expression in our work."

"How nice," I said. "It'll be interesting to see what the judges think of stylized white palm trees in the context of an eighteenth-century historic district."

"Won't it though," he said.

CHAPTER 3

Trader Bob's Treasure Trove Auction House is a grandiose name for what is, in reality, a converted chicken house on a dead-end street on the outskirts of the tiny town of Hardeeville, South Carolina, just across the Talmadge Memorial Bridge from Savannah.

Because Trader Bob, aka Bob Gross, doesn't usually believe in wasting time or money on a catalog or advance flyer, a Trader Bob auction is always an adventure. Some days he'll have a container load of fine English or Dutch antiques, mixed in with odd lots of tube socks and bootleg videos bought from distressed merchandise brokers. More than once I've arrived at Trader Bob's to find him hammering down cases of half-thawed frozen pizzas and slightly dented cans of off-brand pineapple.

But on this December morning, the parking lot, nothing more than a mowed cornfield, was only half full of the usual assortment of dealers' vans and trucks, which was fine by me. Fewer dealers should mean lower bids and better deals.

I was greeted at the door by Leuveda Garner, Bob's sister and business partner, with a friendly nod and a proffered cardboard bid paddle.

"Hey, Weezie," she said. "Long time, no see."

"Merry Christmas, Leuveda," I said. "Got anything good today?"

"Are you in the market for refrigerated dairy cases? Bob bought out a Piggly Wiggly grocery store over in Easley. We've got a bunch of old fixtures and display racks. There's a couple good cash registers you might be interested in."

"I was thinking more of antiques. Is everything going to be store stuff?"

"Not all of it," she said quickly. "We got everything from the owner's estate, too. Some furniture, dishes, linens, all the junk from the attic and basement, and from a couple of barns on the property too." She wrinkled her nose. "Old crap like you like, Weezie. Better go find a chair. Bob's starting early today because he's driving to Hendersonville tonight to pick up a load of furniture, and we heard there's rough weather in the mountains."

Sure enough, as my eyes got accustomed to the dim light of the chicken house, I saw Bob standing at his podium, microphone clipped to his shirtfront, holding aloft a life-size cardboard cutout of the Birds Eye Jolly Green Giant.

"All right now," Bob chanted. "I need a giant bid to start us off. Folks, this is vintage advertising art. Whadya give now? Whadya give? Gimme a hundred. Let's go, ho, ho, ho. Get it?"

The audience groaned, but they got it, all right.

With no time to stroll the merchandise, I picked a folding metal chair down close to the front and did my best to eyeball the offerings from there. Some auctioneers don't mind if you shop while they talk, but Bob Gross runs a tight ship, and he doesn't like any distractions once he starts working.

As Leuveda had promised, there was an entire small grocery store's worth of fixtures and display racks lined up on both sides of the chicken house walls. My eyes locked tight on a battered red-wire three-shelf bread display rack with a tin Sunbeam bread sign affixed to the top. The Sunbeam girl's topknot of golden curls still shone bright as she bit into a slice of white bread. It would be just the thing for a display fixture at Maisie's Daisy. I could already envision it piled with stacks of old quilts, tablecloths, and bed linens.

Right beside the Sunbeam girl leaned an old turquoise painted wooden screen door, with a bright yellow Nehi orange soft-drink metal-door-push advertisement.

"Mine," I whispered to myself. Again I lusted after the screen door for myself. I could already see it as a kitchen door for my own town house on Charlton Street.

I looked nervously around at the other auction-goers to size up the competition, and was elated to see that most of them seemed genuinely interested only in the more modern fixtures Bob was rapidly auctioning off.

When the Sunbeam bread rack came up half an hour later, Bob started the bidding at two hundred dollars. I kept my paddle down. Way too high, I thought. Today, with this thinned-out crowd, he'd be lucky to get fifty bucks, the price I had already budgeted spending on it.

"Two hundred?" Bob implored, searching the room for a bidder. "How 'bout one seventy-five?" He held his arms wide in disbelief. "Folks, this is Americana. You can't put a price on Americana."

"One hundred eighty." The voice came from the back of the room, and I'd heard it recently. Only this morning, to be exact. I whirled around in my chair to see Manny Alvarez, frantically waving his bid paddle.

"That's more like it," Bob said approvingly. "A man who knows values."

Manny Alvarez! What was he doing slumming over here in Hardeeville? I'd been buying from Trader Bob's for years and I'd never seen any other Savannah antiques dealers make the trek over to my secret source before. Had Manny followed my truck over the bridge?

"We've got one eighty," Bob said jovially, looking around the room. "Anybody else?"

My fingers turned white as I gripped the paddle. A hundred and eighty was actually a fair price for the bread rack, cheap even. But I hadn't budgeted spending that kind of money for something I had no intention of selling.

"One eighty going once," Bob droned, staring directly at me. "Weezie Foley, I can't believe you're not bidding on this thing. I thought of you as soon as I saw that little Sunbeam gal."

"One eighty-five," I said through gritted teeth.

"One ninety," Manny fired back.

My heart sped up. "One ninety-two?"

Bob rolled his eyes but nodded, accepting my chintzy raised bid.

"Oh for God's sake," Manny said. "Two hundred."

Bob cut his eyes in my direction. My paddle stayed where it was. Christmas was coming. I had gifts to buy. Bills to pay. The commode in the shop was making weird gurgling noises that foretold a high-priced plumbing problem.

Bob looked at Manny. I looked at Manny. He had his checkbook out, and a smug nonny-nonny-boo-boo expression on his face. I hate smug. But I hate broke worse.

"I'm out," I said, shaking my head.

"You sure?" Bob asked, his gavel poised midair.

I nodded.

"Sold for two hundred dollars," Bob said. "You got yourself a great buy, mister."

"I know," Manny said. He gave me a broad wink and went over to Leuveda to cash out.

I turned around and tried to concentrate on the rest of the auction, consoling myself that I would probably have no competition for the screen door with the Nehi advertisement.

The screen door was a twelve-dollar steal, for which I gave myself a pat on the back, but my paddle stayed in my lap after that, as Bob auctioned off the rest of the Piggly Wiggly people's earthly belongings, which included an astonishing amount of Tupperware containers, Beta format videotapes, and case after case of empty canning jars.

Finally Bob paused to take a swig of coffee from his Styrofoam cup. He glanced down at his watch, and at the greatly diminished crowd of bidders.

"Folks, it's getting late, and I gotta head for the hills. Tell you what. I got three mixed box lots here. We don't have time to drag the stuff out of 'em. Leuveda," he called toward the back of the room. "Hon, tell 'em what all's in these boxes."

Leuveda stood up and ran her hand through her sandy blond curls. "Bob, there's good stuff in there. Some nice old glass Christmas ornaments, some vintage linens. I think there was at least one Christmas tablecloth, and some old aprons and things. Miscellaneous pieces of china, and a jewelry box full of odds and ends. The family took all the really good stuff. But there's probably some good old costume jewelry left."

Bob nodded approvingly and Leuveda took her seat again and resumed cashing out the dealers who were preparing to leave.

"Gimme twenty—one money for all three boxes," Bob urged.

Two men in the front row got up, stretched, and started toward the door.

"Twenty," Bob repeated. "Leuveda, didn't you say those ornaments were Shiny-Brites? Still in the original boxes?"

"Four, maybe five Shiny-Brite boxes," Leuveda agreed, not looking up from her adding machine. "There's a strand of bubble lights too."

My pulse blipped upward. I've collected old glass ornaments for years, and Shiny-Brites—especially in their original boxes—were at the head of my want list.

But before I could say anything, a skinny redheaded woman in front of me cocked her head to one side. "Give you five bucks, Bob."

"Five," he howled. "You can't buy a single Shiny-Brite for that."

"Five," she repeated, standing up.

"Weezie?" he said, noticing my fidgeting.

He had me and he knew it. "Seven," I said, mentally crossing my fingers while trying to keep a poker face.

"Estelle?" He went back to the redhead. "You gonna let her get away with that?"

She shook her head resolutely.

Bob sighed. "You're killing me. Seven once, twice, sold for seven dollars."

I smiled and waved my paddle number at him, which he called out to Leuveda, who'd already added it to my total.

"I gotta get out of this business," Bob said, shaking his head in disgust.

It was nearly four by the time I got the truck loaded. BeBe, I knew, would be champing at the bit to be relieved at the shop. Still I couldn't resist peeking inside the heaviest of the cardboard boxes as I loaded them in the bed of the pickup alongside the screen door.

The bitter loss of the Sunbeam bread rack to Manny Alvarez was quickly forgotten as I lifted out four yellowed cardboard boxes of Shiny-Brite glass ornaments in their original cartons.

"Yes!" I exclaimed, peering inside the brittle cellophane box-top window at the glittering colored glass orbs. The boxes contained not just unadorned round balls, but rarer, and more desirable, glass figural ornaments in the shapes of angels, snowmen, and Santas. Some had flocked swirls or stripes, and a few were kugel and teardrop shaped. Each box held a dozen ornaments, and all were in fifties colors like turquoise, pink, pale blue, and mint green.

I never bother to read price guides for the things I collect, because these days I buy only when the price is cheap, and I'm never looking to resell, but still, even I knew my seven-dollar purchase was a winner.

Beneath the boxes of ornaments, I unwrapped a neatly folded, if slightly stained, fifties Christmas bridge cloth, with decorative borders of red and green holly leaves interspersed with playing card motifs. There were eight kitchen aprons, all with Christmas themes, ranging from practical red-and-white gingham and rickrack numbers to a flirty red ruffled chiffon number to a starched white organza one with hand-crocheted lace edging and an appliquéd snowflake pocket.

"Adorable," I said, happily patting the pile of aprons. Beneath them I found a cardboard box filled with dozens of delicate vintage lady's handkerchiefs, and beneath the aprons, I found the jewelry box Leuveda had promised.

The box itself was nothing special. I'd seen dozens of embossed leather boxes like this one at yard sales and thrift stores over the years. Inside I found the expected jumble of old glass beads, discolored strands of cheap pearls, orphaned clip-on earrings, and inexpensive dime-store bracelets and brooches.

I rifled the jewelry jumble in the bottom of the box with my forefinger, like a painter stirring paint, until something sharp jabbed me, drawing blood.

"Oww!" I exclaimed, sucking my wounded finger. With my left hand I picked up the piece that had stuck me.

It was a brooch. A big, gaudy blue-jeweled brooch, maybe two inches high, in the shape of a Christmas tree. A blue Christmas tree.

My cell phone rang. I looked at the caller ID panel and winced. BeBe. Time was up. She was tired of playing store, I knew. Anyway, I had to get back and finish decorating the shop before getting ready to go hit the holiday party circuit tonight.

"Hi," I said, cradling the phone between my ear and shoulder as I pinned the brooch to my blouse. "How's business?"

"Great," BeBe said unenthusiastically. "Your dog drooled on my shoe. Your toilet sounds like it's going to explode. But all is not lost. I sold that ugly brown stick-looking table by the door for two hundred fifty dollars."

"You what?" I exclaimed.

"Yeah, I couldn't believe it either," she said, laughing. "And I got cash, so don't worry about the check bouncing."

"Two hundred and fifty," I repeated dumbly.

"Great, huh?"

"Not so much," I told her. "That was a signed, handmade Jimmy Beeson hickory-stick table from the 1920s. It came out of one of those old lake lodges up at Lake Rabun in North Georgia. I paid almost a thousand for it myself."

"Oh," BeBe said. "So marking it two hundred fifty dollars was kind of a loss leader thing?"

"No," I said sadly. "The price tag was twenty-five hundred dollars. Two zeroes."

"Whoopsie," BeBe said. "Look, I'll make it right with you when I see you. But I've got to lock up and go get ready for your uncle's party tonight. Is it all right to leave Jethro alone until you get here?"

"Go ahead on," I said. "He used to like to chew on the leg of that table. But that's not a problem anymore."

CHAPTER 4

When I got back to Maisie's Daisy, I parked the truck and walked across the street to get a better perspective of the shop's decorations. The fruit garlands and topiaries were tasteful and by the book. And yes, I thought ruefully, Manny was right. BOR-RING!

But rules were rules. And if I wanted to win the historic district decorating contest, I'd just have to be a by-the-book kind of girl.

As I ferried my auction finds from the truck to the shop, an idea came to me. The outside of my shop might have to look like Williamsburg proper, but the inside of the shop could be anything I liked. And that box of vintage Christmas stuff had put me in a funky kind of mood.

I switched on the shop lights, and Jethro ran to my side, planting his big black-and-white paws on my chest. "Not now, sport," I said, giving him a quick scratch behind the ears. I went over to the pine armoire that hid the shop's sound system and flipped through my collection of Christmas CDs, passing on the tasteful instrumentals, the Harry Connick, Nat King Cole, and Johnny Mathis selections.

"Here," I said aloud, sliding a CD into the player. "Here's what I'm in the mood for."

It was my all-time favorite Christmas compilation, *A Christmas Gift for You from Phil Spector*, featuring all the legendary (and nutty) sixties producer's acts: the Crystals, the Ronettes, Darlene Love, even the inimitable Bob B. Soxx and the Blue Jeans.

A moment later, Darlene Love's powerful voice swung into "White Christmas," done in Phil Spector's trademark "wall of sound" style, sounding nothing like Bing Crosby, but just right in her own way.

I picked up the boxes of Shiny-Brites and headed for the display window. For the past few years, I'd been buying every aluminum Christmas tree I could find at yard sales and flea markets, but the rest of the world had gotten hip to fifties, or midcentury modern as it was now called, and the trees had become expensive and scarce. This year I'd managed to scrounge only three trees, and I'd had to turn down dozens of customers who wanted to buy them out of my window. Now I flitted from tree to tree, placing the Shiny-Brites on the window side of the trees, where they could be seen by passersby. I interspersed the vintage balls with newer, reproduction ornaments I'd ordered at the Atlanta gift mart in September. With the tiny white flicker lights, they were glittery and wonderful.

But the window was still too stiff, too formal. I'd created a living room vignette, with a pair of red tartan–slipcovered armchairs, a primitive fireplace mantel and surround with peeling green paint, and a red-and-green hand-hooked rug. A twig table held a stack of old leather-bound books, including an opened copy of Clement Clarke Moore's *'Twas the Night Before Christmas* with illustrations by N. C. Wyeth.

I'd thought the window perfect only a few hours ago, but now it seemed way too safe and predictable.

I crossed my arms over my chest and gave it some thought. Suddenly the Ronettes swung into "Frosty the Snowman," and I got inspired.

I moved the twig table and replaced it with a just-purchased could-be Stickley library table. An improvement, I decided. Reluctantly, I brought out my stack of dime-store Christmas gift boxes. I'd have to fight my customers to keep them to myself, but really, they were too wonderful not to put on display. I arranged them under the tree and took another critical look. It needed more. Much more.

Glancing at my watch, I realized I'd lost track of time. The party started at seven, and Daniel was supposed to pick me up in fifteen minutes!

Later, I promised myself. Genius can't be rushed. I whistled for Jethro, picked up the box of costume jewelry from the auction, and hurried over to my house.

As always, when I stepped inside my front door, I said a silent prayer of thanks. Mine was not the grandest, oldest house in the historic district, or even on Charlton Street. It was built in 1858 and had austere lines. But it was made of coveted Savannah gray brick, had beautiful lacy wrought-iron trim, a wonderful courtyard garden, and a fantastic gourmet kitchen of my own design. And it was mine. All mine. I'd found the house when Tal and I were still newlyweds. The $200,000 price tag was more money than we could afford, but I wrote the down payment check without a second thought, and plunged into remodeling it, doing much of the work myself.

This house was my anchor. My dream. It had outlasted the marriage to Tal. He'd been awarded the town house in our divorce settlement, and I'd only gotten the carriage house. But through a strange turn of events, Tal's fortunes had taken a dive, and he'd needed to sell the town house. I was overjoyed to buy him out. And when my antiques business started to take off, I'd been able to buy the twin to my town house next door. I moved Maisie's Daisy out of the carriage house and into the ground floor of that house and rented out the top two floors to a young couple who both taught at the art school.

After bribing Jethro with a dog biscuit, I bolted upstairs to dress for the party. Earlier in the day I'd laid out a simple pair of black capris and a black lace top to wear. But the blue Christmas tree pin had made me rethink my outfit.

Only vintage would match my mood tonight. Once I was out of the shower, I rifled through my closet, looking for the right combination.

Aha! But could I still get in it?

The black fifties cocktail dress was one I'd found at a great vintage shop in Atlanta called Frock of Ages. It usually killed me to pay retail for old stuff, but when I'd spotted this dress in the shop window one Saturday while cruising down McLendon Avenue, I knew I had to have it. Even at forty bucks.

The bodice was beaded black brocade, with a deeply scooped neck and cap sleeves, and the full, ankle-length bouffant skirt was black chiffon over two layers of black tulle crinoline. I spritzed my neck and breasts with my favorite perfume, then struggled into a black waist-cinching Merry Widow, stepped into the dress, sucked in my breath, and struggled with the zipper. When the dress was still at half-mast, I heard the doorbell ringing downstairs and Jethro barking.

Damn. True, it was ten after seven, but Daniel was never on time these days. His restaurant, Guale, was always swamped at the holidays, and since he'd bought out BeBe's interest in it, he seemed to work longer and longer hours. I hadn't even put on makeup or fixed my hair properly, but it wouldn't do to keep Daniel waiting.

Not this time of year. Christmas seemed to make him grumpy. I knew it was because he was overworked, but it still made me a little sad that he couldn't enjoy what should have been a happy holiday.

Especially this year. My business was doing well, and after all those years of working as a chef in other people's kitchens, Daniel had finally realized his dream of owning his own restaurant. After three years of dating, I had secretly halfway convinced myself that this Christmas could be the one. . . .

I ran downstairs to answer the door. He stood on the doorstep, key out, with a funny look on his face.

"What's wrong?" I gave him a quick kiss.

"Nothing," he said, glancing around at the street behind. "I was going to let myself in, but I had the eeriest feeling just now. Like I was being watched."

I poked my head out the door and looked up and down the street. I saw a flash of red disappearing through the square.

"Maybe you *were* being watched," I said, drawing him inside. "I bet it was those creeps Manny and Cookie."

"Who?" Daniel asked, kissing my neck. "Mmm. You smell good." He held me at arm's length and smiled. "Looking good too. I don't suppose that's a new dress?"

"New in 1958, I think," I said, twirling so he could get the full effect.

"Could you zip me, please?" I asked, holding my hair off my neck. "Manny and Cookie own Babalu, that new shop across the square, over on Harris. They're trying to put me out of business. I think they were probably over here spying, checking on my decorations for the business district Christmas decoration contest."

He zipped me up without any funny business. So I knew he was distracted.

"What makes you think they're trying to put you out of business?" he asked.

"Everything. But don't get me started. I just have to run upstairs and slap on some makeup, and I'll be ready to go."

"You look fine to me," Daniel said. "Anyway, we really need to get a move on here, Weezie. I've got to go back to the restaurant in a couple hours. We've got two law firm

Christmas parties tonight, and the partners all expect the owner to put in an appearance."

"Daniel!" I protested. "It's James and Jonathan 's first party. You can't cut out early. And I don't want to."

"You can stay," he said. "But there's no way I can. Now, can we get going?"

"One minute," I promised.

Upstairs, I dabbed on some eyeliner, mascara, and lipstick, and slipped into a pair of black velvet high-heeled pumps. I grabbed my black velvet shawl, wrapped it around my shoulders, and fastened the blue Christmas tree pin to it.

"Ready," I said, still breathless on the bottom stair.

Daniel picked up my house keys and handed them to me. He looked at me and frowned.

"What?" I asked, tugging the neckline of the dress. "Are my boobs falling out again?"

"No," he said slowly. He reached out and touched my shawl.

"This pin. Where did you get it?"

"At Trader Bob's auction today," I said, surprised. Even though he's a chef, and more arty than most, Daniel is all man. He rarely notices things like jewelry or shoes. "Why? Don't you like it?"

"Yeah. It's fine," he said, still staring at the pin.

"What? You're still staring."

"My mother had a pin just like that," he said, looking away. "My brothers and I pooled our lawn-mowing money and bought it for her the year my dad left. She used to wear it, every Christmas. She said it was appropriate. You know, because my dad left, we were all having a blue Christmas that year. Like the Elvis Presley song."

"Oh," I said softly. Daniel never talked about his mother. Or his father, for that matter. I knew that his dad abandoned his mom and their three sons when Daniel was just a kid. I also knew that Daniel's mom, Paula, had wound up in a scandal involving her married boss at the sugar refinery here in Savannah, where she worked. When the dust settled, the executive had been sent to a federal prison in Florida, but not before he divorced his wife and married Paula. Not long after that, Paula Stipanek Gambrell had followed her new husband to Florida. Daniel and his two older brothers had been raised by his aunt Lucy. It was not a happy story.

I tucked my arm into his. "If you guys bought a pin like this, it just proves you had great taste. These pins were quite the craze from the forties through the sixties, although not so much in the war years, because metal was hard to get for jewelry. I've seen hundreds of variations of Christmas tree pins. Every costume jewelry company made them. Coro, Carolee, Trifari, you name it. And some of the more expensive ones that were sold in jewelry or department stores, signed pieces made by Weiss or Eisenberg or Miriam Haskell, sell for hundreds of dollars now."

Daniel gave a short, humorless laugh. "Yeah, well, I can guarantee you that one ain't worth hundreds. We bought my mom's pin at the Kress five-and-dime on Broughton Street. Between us, we scraped up maybe five bucks to pay for it."

As we walked to Daniel's truck, I heard Jethro give a plaintive howl from inside the house.

"Poor guy. He hates staying home alone."

Daniel tugged at his tie, a rare concession on his part. "Yeah, well, I'd gladly trade places with him tonight."

"Thanks!" I said sharply.

"Sorry," he said, giving me a conciliatory peck on the cheek. "I just really don't get into Christmas parties. Never have. But what I should have said was, I wish you and I were staying home tonight. Just the two of us. I'd love to help you get out of that new dress of yours."

"Hmmph," I said, unconvinced.

CHAPTER 5

Shortly after celebrating his silver jubilee in the priesthood, my uncle James hung up his clerical collar and came home to Savannah to practice law and live a quiet life in the modest house he inherited from his mother. Not long after that, he timidly snuck out of the closet, and not long after that, met his current partner, Jonathan McDowell.

My conservative uncle had waited three long years before finally giving in to Jonathan's request that they live together openly. In September, Jonathan, a charming, forty-five-year-old assistant district attorney, and his adorable mother, Miss Sudie, had moved in to James's house on Washington Avenue.

Tonight would be their first party. For weeks, James had been as nervous as a cat in a room full of rocking chairs. "What if nobody comes?" he'd fretted as we'd gone over the menu for the open house "drop-in."

"People will come," I'd promised. "You and Jonathan have

lots of friends. And everybody loves Miss Sudie. And besides," I'd said, "people are dying to see what Jonathan has done with your house."

James shook his head and ran his fingers through his thinning hair. "He's painted the living room brown, you know. Brown! My mother would be rolling in her grave if she knew. She always kept the downstairs rooms pink."

I shuddered. "Pepto-Bismol pink. Old lady colors. Anyway, it's not really brown now. It's a dark mocha. And it's wonderful. Jonathan has divine taste. And I'm so glad he talked you into getting rid of that horrible old stuff of grandmother's."

"I thought you liked antiques," James said.

"Not all antiques were created equal," I informed him. "That horrid pink velvet sofa was butt ugly, and you know it. And those baby-blue tufted armchairs . . .yeecchh."

"The new sofa is really comfortable," James admitted. "And Jonathan's leather armchairs are great for reading. And he did let me keep the stuff in my bedroom."

So tonight was my uncle's coming-out party. In more ways than one. As we approached his house, I happily noted that the old house was aglow with Chistmas lights, with a big evergreen wreath on the front door and half a dozen people standing on the front porch sipping wine and chatting. And both sides of the street were lined with cars.

"James was afraid nobody would show up," I told Daniel, directing him to pull into the driveway behind my father's dark gray Buick. "Mama and Daddy never stay out past eight," I reminded him.

Daniel glanced over at me. "So your mother's okay with them living together? She wasn't shocked?"

"I wouldn't say she actually approved," I said. "But you know what a snob Mama is. The McDowells are old Savannah money. She's thrilled that James is seeing somebody of quality. And she adores Miss Sudie."

James met us at the front door, resplendent in a snappy hunter-green plaid sport coat and a rust-colored turtleneck sweater.

"Wow!" I said, kissing him. "You're right out of a Ralph Lauren magazine ad."

He frowned. "Is that good?"

"Very good," I said with a laugh. "And you didn't even have to put on a tie."

"Not even for Jonathan," James said. "Not even for Christmas."

Jonathan walked up and slung an arm around my shoulder and Daniel's. "Is he complaining about the damned brown paint again?"

"No," I said. "He's congratulating himself on not having to wear a necktie."

"Well, come on in and get something to eat and drink," Jonathan said. "Daniel did an amazing job with the food. Those baby lamb chops are to die for."

"Thanks," Daniel said.

"Just don't mention the cost to James," Jonathan said. "He still thinks cocktail wienies and Cheez Whiz are perfectly acceptable party food."

"It's the Foley family curse," I told Jonathan. "We're all so tight we squeak when we walk."

While Daniel went into the kitchen to check on the food, I circulated around, chatting with friends and family.

I found Mama and Daddy seated in the living room, Daddy, looking uncomfortable in his good suit, and Mama wearing her traditional Christmas party outfit, which consisted of a green wool skirt and one of those awful seasonal sweaters she adores—this one featured giant knitted Christmas trees adorned with tiny ornaments that actually lit up and blinked. Unfortunately, two of the blinking red lights were located directly in the middle of her chest, so that from across the room it appeared that her nipples were winking.

"Weezie," Mama said, reaching out to pull me down beside her on the sofa. "Don't you look nice tonight!"

I glanced down at my dress and tugged at the neckline. Old habits die hard. "Really? You like this dress?" Mama usually hates my vintage clothes. She can't understand how I could stand to wear what she calls "dead people's cast-offs."

"The pin," Mama said, reaching out and touching the Christmas tree fastened to my stole. "I had a pin like this when you were little. Do you remember?"

I looked down at the pin. "Just like this one?"

She frowned. "Well, no. Mine was sort of gold, with branches, and there were all different colors of pearls on it."

"Pins like this were really popular years ago," I told her. "Daniel says his mother had a pin exactly like this one. It was blue and everything."

"Ohhh," Mama said. She had a long memory for scandal and remembered everything about the Hoyt Gambrell trial. "Does he ever hear from his mother?"

"No," I said briefly, already regretting I'd brought up the subject.

"Where is Daniel?" Daddy asked. "Working at the restaurant, is he?"

"He's here," I said. "Guale's catering the food tonight, you know."

"Nice," Mama said vaguely. "What do you call that mushy rice stuff they're serving with the lamb chops?"

"Risotto?"

"Interesting," Mama said, and then brightening, added, "I brought James one of my famous fruitcakes to serve for dessert. Don't forget to try a slice."

"I won't," I said, secretly vowing to avoid the cake like the plague. My mother had been a closet alcoholic for most of my life, but after she'd gone through rehab, she'd turned her newfound energy to cooking. Unfortunately, sobriety did nothing to improve her culinary skills.

"I've added something new to my fruitcake this year," Mama confided. Lowering her voice and covering her mouth with her hand, lest someone try to steal her secret ingredient, she whispered it.

"Maple syrup!"

"Really?"

Daddy nodded sadly. "She like to run the IGA out of Aunt Jemima's."

"Two dozen cakes," Mama reported. "It's a new record. I've got yours out in the car, if you want to follow us out when we get ready to leave."

"I'll do that," I promised, getting up. "Well, I better check in with Daniel. He's got to leave early and get back to the restaurant. They've got a couple of big private parties tonight, and he has to put in an appearance."

"Don't forget about the cake, now," Mama chirped. "I've only got a dozen left. They're a big hit this year."

What, I wondered as I drifted through the rooms, alive with light and laughter, could people be doing with maple-syrup-flavored fruitcakes?

Doorstops. Boat anchors. Bookends.

I found Daniel in the dining room, sprinkling chopped parsley on a chafing dish full of shrimp gumbo.

"Looking good," I said, giving him a quick kiss.

"You too," he said absentmindedly.

"Something wrong?" I asked, knowing already that something was.

"There should be a bowl of trifle on the sideboard over there," he said, pointing at my grandmother's massive mahogany server. "It was in the kitchen when I first got here, but it's gone now."

"Everybody loves your trifle," I said. "Maybe people just scarfed it all up."

He shook his head. "No. There were two whole bowls of it in the kitchen. We made enough to serve a hundred. Should have been plenty. And the bowls are gone too."

"Really?" I went over to the sideboard to investigate. Beside a cut crystal bowl of punch I spotted a silver tray layered with slice after slice of fruitcake. Maple scented.

"Case closed," I said, reporting back to Daniel. "Marian Foley strikes again."

"Your mother ate a whole bowl of trifle?"

"I doubt it," I said. "Yours is afloat in sherry. Mama's terri-fied of falling off the wagon. She won't even take cough syrup anymore. No, I suspect Mama did away with your trifle because it was competing with her fruitcake."

"No!" Daniel said. "So that's where that cake came from? I thought it was a gift from one of James's clients."

"Afraid not. She told me herself that she'd brought one for the party. That fruitcake is her pride and joy."

Daniel went over to the aforementioned tray, bent down and sniffed, and grimaced.

"What the hell?"

"Family secret," I said, crossing my heart. "I've been sworn to silence."

"Dueling desserts," Daniel said. "Only the Foleys."

"I'm sorry," I told him. "Do you want me to see if I can fig-ure out what she did with the trifle?"

"No," he said. "Let James deal with it. Listen, sweetie, I hate to mention it, but I've really got to get over to Guale."

"Already?" I checked my watch. "It's only a little after eight."

"You could stay," he suggested. "Get your parents to take you home."

"Never mind. Let's find James and Jon and say good night."

He headed toward the living room, but I pulled him back. "Not there. I've got to sneak out without Mama seeing me. There's a fruitcake with my name on it out in Daddy's car."

"Ow," he said. "I hope he left the windows rolled down."

Daniel was quiet as we rode home.

"You okay?" I asked, scooting over and rubbing his neck.

"Just tired," he said.

"That's all?"

"It's a busy time of year," Daniel said. "There's a lot more involved in owning a restaurant than there is in just cooking."

"I know. But there's something else going on too, isn't there?"

He sighed. "I hate Christmas."

"Daniel!"

"It's no big deal. In two weeks, it'll all be over. Life can get back to normal."

"This should be a happy time of year. I'm busy too, but I love Christmas. I love everything about it. . . ."

"That's you," he said abruptly. "Not me."

I sighed. "Anything I can do to help? Do you want to talk about it?"

He shot me a look of disbelief.

When we got to the house, he parked the truck and left the motor running. "You can't come in, even for a minute?" I asked.

He shook his head and walked me to my front stoop. He took his keys out and unlocked the door. "I'll call you later," he said, opening the door wide.

Before I could say anything, Jethro came bounding out. He was gone in a flash.

"Jethro!" I screamed. "Jethro, come back!"

"Damned dog," Daniel muttered. He stepped out onto the sidewalk. "Here, boy," he called. "Here, Jethro."

His voice echoed on the deserted street. A skinny yellow cat slinked across the square, and I heard an owl hooting from the limb of a nearby tree. But no goofy barking.

I stood in the middle of Charlton Street and yelled his name.

"Jethro!"

"Now what?" Daniel asked, annoyed.

"Just go on and leave," I snapped. "I'll take care of finding the damned dog."

"Get in the truck," Daniel said. "We'll look together."

"No," I said stubbornly. "He's my dog. I'll take my own truck and look for him. Go on to Guale. You're late already."

"All right," Daniel said. He gave me a quick peck on the cheek. "I'll call you, okay? And don't worry. He can't have gone far."

I locked the front door and got in my truck, pitching my high heels onto the floor, and the shawl, which was hard to drive in, on the front seat. I cruised the streets of the district for more than an hour, stopping every block or so, calling his name.

Every person I saw along the way, I stopped and asked if they'd seen a black-and-white dog. But nobody had. I went back to my house and checked the courtyard garden, in hope that my own Lassie had come home. But the gate was locked, and there was no dog.

I got back in my truck and retraced my earlier route, calling for my lost Jethro, trying to reassure myself that he would be safe. He's a city dog, I told myself. I'd found him when he was just a stray puppy, literally in a heap of trash in front of a decaying house in the Victorian district. He could take care of himself. And he was wearing his collar and tag. Somebody would find him and call me.

It was close to midnight when I gave up the hunt and went home. Dejected, I got a blanket and pillow and decided to sleep on the sofa—just in case Jethro came back, and I heard him scratching at the door.

The message light was blinking on my answering machine. I pressed the button and prayed. Maybe Jethro had already been found.

But the caller was Daniel.

"Hey," he said, his voice sounding tired. "Don't be mad at me. We'll find Jethro. Everything will be all right. Call me as soon as you get home."

Fat chance, I thought, tears welling up in my eyes. I pounded my pillow, pulled my quilt over my head, and fell into an uneasy sleep.

CHAPTER 6

Three times during the night, I got up, opened the front door, and looked up and down the street, willing Jethro to materialize there, ears pricked up, tail wagging, tongue lolling from the side of his mouth, big brown eyes begging for a treat. Each time, I dragged myself back to the sofa and tried to sleep.

At seven o'clock, I gave up. I trudged into the kitchen and poured myself a Diet Coke, followed by an ibuprofen chaser. I had no appetite, so I picked at a granola bar before discarding it in the trash.

Flyers, I decided, would be a good idea. I could print them up on my computer and post them around the neighborhood. And at nine, when I figured the county animal shelter probably opened, I would call and see if Jethro had been picked up.

I was in the living room, folding the quilt, when I heard

the faint sound of whining coming from outside. I ran to the front door, opened it, and peered out.

The morning paper was on my front stoop. I looked up and down the street again, but saw nothing. Where was that whining coming from?

Dressed only in my flannel pajama bottoms and a camisole top, I stepped out onto the sidewalk. My truck!

A familiar black-and-white face bobbed up and down in the front seat of my truck, whining and pawing at the window.

"Jethro!" I cried, running over to the curb. I opened the door and he leaped into my arms, licking my face, tail wagging a mile a minute. I laughed until I cried. And two tattooed and body-pierced art students, who happened to be walking by, stopped to enjoy the spectacle of my reunion with my dog.

"Excellent," said the androgynous kid with the purple spiked hair.

"Radical," agreed his/her counterpart, who had a skateboard tucked under his arm.

"How in the world?" I asked, when I was able to speak again. "How did you get in that truck?"

Jethro licked my face in answer. I noticed for the first time that a frayed piece of yellow nylon cord was tied to his collar. Tucking my squirming dog under my arm, I looked inside the truck. A large, damp bone rested on the driver's seat, beside my black velvet shawl, which, judging by the amount of dog hair clinging to it, had been used as a bed during his stay there.

I grabbed the shawl and carried both it and the dog inside.

As soon as we were in the house, he jumped out of my arms and ran into the kitchen. I followed him there and watched with relief as he scarfed down an entire bowl of chow. When he was done, I sat down on the floor and gave him a thorough examination. But he was fine. No scratches, cuts, not a mark on him.

He rolled onto his back and allowed me to give him a welcome-home belly scratch.

"You had me worried sick," I scolded. "How did you get in that truck? Who found you and brought you home?"

Instead of an explanation, he went to the back door and scratched, letting me know it was time for a bathroom break. But before I let him out, I went into the garden first, making sure the gate was securely locked.

Satisfied that Jethro was safely fenced in, I ran upstairs and got dressed in blue jeans and a flannel shirt. I was dying to know where Jethro had spent the night, but my investigation would have to be put on hold. I had a full day ahead of me, finishing my redo of Maisie's Daisy window and getting ready for the open house tonight.

I was hanging up the cocktail dress I'd left in a heap on the bedroom floor when it occurred to me that I'd need to take the velvet shawl to the cleaners. I love my dog, but not his scent. I picked it up to see if there were any visible stains, and to remove the blue Christmas tree pin.

There were no stains, but there was also no pin.

I turned the shawl inside out, to see if it had come unattached, but it was definitely not on the shawl.

I went outside to the truck and ran my hands under the

seats. I searched the floorboards. I even looked in the bed of the truck, which was uncharacteristically empty. Still no pin. But I noticed that the driver's-side window had been cranked down about an inch. I knew with a certainty that I'd had the windows rolled up last night and the heater on, because it had gotten downright chilly once the sun went down. Had I locked the truck?

Usually I did keep the truck locked. An unfortunate side effect of living downtown was that crime was a nagging constant. Over the years, I'd had batteries stolen out of my car, potted plants stolen from my porch, and once somebody had even stolen the gas lamps outside my front door. But I'd been in such a state last night, I couldn't say with a certainty whether or not I had locked the truck.

What was unquestionable was that somebody, sometime during the night, had tethered my dog to that makeshift leash, placed him in the truck, given him a bone for solace, and cracked the window so that he wouldn't suffocate. That same guardian angel had also, apparently, decided to reward himself with my Christmas tree pin.

Fine, I thought. I'd have paid a real, and handsome, cash reward to anybody who'd brought Jethro back home. And I'd have gladly thrown the pin in as a bonus.

Before going back to lock up the house, I walked across the street to take another look at the Christmas decorations on Maisie's Daisy.

What the hell? My daisy had been plucked! The topiary trees were virtually denuded of fruit. Apples, oranges, lemons, limes, even the cunning little kumquats I'd paid an indecent price for, were all gone. The garland around the front door was similarly picked clean. Pieces of popcorn littered the sidewalk, and I felt cranberries squashing under my sneakers. The only fruit left was the pineapple I'd nailed to the plaque above the door, and a couple of random pomegranates.

Without the fruit, the storefront looked naked and pathetic. Had the same thief who'd taken my pin also made off with my fruit? Some crime spree.

"Son of a bitch!" I muttered. Now I'd have to start all over again. With the open house tonight, and the decoration contest judges due at six, there was no time to waste.

Still I wondered if other businesses had also been victimized during the night.

I took a quick hike across Troup Square. Babalu was even more resplendent than it had been yesterday. It was a winter wonderland on steroids. New to the scene was a pair of eight-foot-high snowmen. I had to touch them to make sure they weren't real. Although they glittered like fresh snow, they were actually made of some kind of cotton batting sprayed with iridescent sparkles. The snowmen held aloft shiny black snow shovels crossed over the shop's doorway. Standing outside the shop, I could hear Chrismas music being piped out onto the sidewalk. And yes, as I sniffed hungrily, I realized these men would stop at nothing in their quest for world domination. That was undeniably the scent of fresh-baked gingerbread wafting into the chilly morning air.

The bastards! Manny and Cookie's decorations were breathtakingly intact.

The shop door opened with a merry tinkle, and a small black powder puff with legs emerged. It trotted over to the fire hydrant at the curb, and daintily took a morning pee.

"Good Ruthie!"

Cookie Parker poked his head out the door and looked at me quizzically. "Yes?"

He was wearing a black satin bathrobe, and his chunky white legs ended in a pair of black velvet monogrammed slippers. His dyed blond hair stood up in wisps, and a black satin sleep mask had been pushed up over his forehead.

"I'm Weezie Foley. I own Maisie's Daisy, across the square," I said.

"I'm aware of who you are and what you do," he said coldly. "But what do you want here?"

"Somebody vandalized my decorations last night," I said. "Most of the fruit is gone. And my truck was broken into. I was just checking . . . to see."

"If we'd been hit?" Cookie smiled. "Your concern is touching. But as you can see, nothing here has been touched."

He clapped his hands smartly. "Come, Ruthie." The little dog trotted down the sidewalk a few yards and looked back at Cookie, as if taunting him.

"Naughty girl," Cookie said, shaking his finger at the dog. "Come along now. It's cold out here. You need your sweater if we're going to take a walk. And I need some pants."

"You didn't happen to see anybody suspicious last night, did you?" I asked.

"No more so than usual. Just the usual avant-garde types who wander the streets at night," he said. "Ruthie!" He clapped his hands again, rapidly. "Come right here, right this minute, miss."

"Odd that my decorations were trashed, and yet yours weren't touched," I commented.

"Maybe it was the birds. Damned pigeons!" Cookie suggested.

"Pigeons that carry off oranges and apples? I doubt it."

The dog trotted farther down the sidewalk, and I did the same.

"Pricks," I muttered to myself. It was way too much of a coincidence that my decorations had been pilfered, while Babalu remained untouched.

But I had no proof that Cookie and Manny were the culprits, and no time to look for any other suspects.

Instead I went home, got Jethro, and went to work at Maisie's Daisy.

First thing, I stripped off the grapevines and what was left of the popcorn strings. I took down the pineapple plaque too. Now that I had a clean slate, I could think again. But it was nearly ten o'clock. Where was I going to come up with natural, vernacular Christmas decorations—prizewinning decorations, this late in the game?"

I sat down in one of the plaid armchairs in the window and closed my eyes. A minute later, I jumped up and loaded the CD player with Christmas albums. I put on all the good stuff: the Phil Spector compilation, Elvis, another compilation I'd gotten at Old Navy, and a couple of CDs from a Rhino Records promotion I'd ordered off the Internet. I hit shuffle and sat down and waited for inspiration.

As luck would have it, the first song was the Ronettes version of "I Saw Mommy Kissing Santa Claus."

For some reason, I thought instantly of Daniel's mom, Paula Gambrell. Had Daniel ever, I wondered, crept downstairs like the kid in the song, and thought he'd seen his mother kissing Santa Claus? Did he have any good memories at all of his parents? I'd probably never know. Family just wasn't something Daniel liked to discuss.

When the next song started, I laughed out loud. Eartha Kitt singing "Santa Baby." In it, the sultry gold digger implores a Sugar Daddy Santa Baby to bring an impressive list of luxury gifts; a fur coat, a '54 convertible—light blue—a duplex, checks, decorations for her tree, bought at Tif-fa-ny—and especially, a ring, meaning bling.

Before I knew it, I was up and vamping around the shop, swishing an imaginary feather boa and humming along with Eartha.

But it wasn't until Elvis came on that I had my brainstorm.

Blue Christmas!

Screw the fruits and nuts. Screw vernacular. Screw tasteful. Screw the judges and the rules! I was gonna have a blue Christmas this year. And I'd by God have fun doing it.

CHAPTER 7

Blue, blue, blue, I chanted as I drove around town in a last-minute shopping spree. And maybe some silver. Yes, definitely silver. I hit Target and in the seasonal aisle loaded up on plain silver and metallic-blue glass tree ornaments. I bought boxes and boxes of silver garland, aluminum tinsel, and ten strands of old-fashioned-looking big bulb lights, all in blue, of course, to supplement the white twinkle lights I already had at home. Thank God the big box stores had discovered retro!

At Hancock Fabrics, my mind was reeling with songs with blue in the title. I heard Bobby Vinton singing "Blue Velvet," Diane Renay singing "Navy Blue," Willie Nelson crooning "Blue Eyes Crying in the Rain," even Elvis doing "Blue Hawaii."

My hands trailed across the racks of fabrics. I'd need a big effect for just a few bucks. Regretfully, I turned away from a bolt of midnight blue velveteen—at $14.99 a yard, it was way too pricey. Blue satin was out of the question, and blue denim, still too high at $7.99 a yard, was too modern for the look I was going for.

But at the back of the store, in the bridal department, I hit pay dirt. Tulle! At eighty-eight cents a yard the price was right. But the colors—white, green, and red, were all wrong.

Still, I thought, eighty-eight cents a yard! I grabbed four bolts of the white tulle, all they had, and headed for the cash register, grabbing a bottle of blue Rit dye on the way.

At home I loaded the washing machine with what seemed like miles of netting, and spun the regulator dial to the gentle cycle. As the tub filled with water, I carefully added half a cap of blue dye, then a capful, then throwing caution to the wind, I went for two capfuls.

Blue foam filled the tub. I let the wash cycle run for only five minutes before manually switching to the machine's rinse and then spin cycle.

As soon as the machine slowed, I jerked open the lid of the washer. Blue! I had a gorgeous wet glop of bright blue tulle, which I unceremoniously dumped into the dryer, also set for the gentle cycle.

But I had no time to waste sitting by the dryer.

Back at Maisie's Daisy, I stripped the shop's window of everything but the aluminum Christmas trees, trimmed with my hoard of Shiny-Brite ornaments and the tiny white twinkle lights. I draped the big blue bulbs in swags across the front of the window.

Then I lugged the shop's one display bed, a vintage white

iron twin bed, and set it up in the window, draped with a white chenille bedspread with bright blue and green peacocks. I added a pile of pillows stuffed into old pillowcases trimmed in crocheted lace, and stepped back to study the effect. Not bad.

In the stockroom, I rummaged around until I found the big old "portable" record player I'd picked up at an estate sale, along with the funny round black record caddy I'd found at another sale, still full of some long-ago teenager's collection of 45s. I had my own stash of albums, 78s, that I'd collected just for the album covers. I set the record player up on the floor at the foot of the bed and fanned the 45s and the albums around the record player.

I studied my vignette. It was cute, yes. But it wasn't telling me anything. I needed story. I needed drama. I needed teen angst.

Back to the stockroom. I found a pile of old magazines that I had kept because I liked the graphics and the illustrations. There was a sixties issue of *Look* magazine with Jackie Kennedy on the cover. Too modern. Several old copies of *The Saturday Evening Post* with Norman Rockwell illustrations. Too corny. Half a dozen copies of Archie comics. Yes! I'd always identified with Betty, hated Veronica. I passed over some *TV Guides* and some great *Field & Streams* from the forties, till I came to the bottom of the stack, where my quest was rewarded with three like-new copies of *Silver Screen* magazine from 1958. The lurid headlines about Marilyn Monroe, Lana Turner, and Tab Hunter would be just the thing for my teen tableau.

As I was gathering up the magazines, I spied a pink

princess telephone. Pink was a prized color for a princess phone, but I frowned. Wrong color for a blue Christmas.

I could spray-paint it blue, but that would ruin the resale value, which was around sixty dollars. I turned the phone over and found the scrap of masking tape with the price I'd paid for it. Fifty cents.

My honor was at stake here. I took the phone out into the alley behind the shop, set it on an old copy of the *Savannah Morning News*, and quickly created an adorable, if now worthless, powder blue princess phone.

It was time to check on my dye job. The blue netting was absolutely heavenly. I gathered it up in my arms and was on my way out the back door when I spotted one of the many silver-framed photos of family and friends I had scattered all over the town house. This particular picture was of me and Daniel at the beach. I scowled at Daniel. He hadn't even called yet to find out if Jethro was all right.

Looking at the picture of my boyfriend took me right back to my own teenage angst. I turned the frame over and slipped the picture out of the frame, leaving it on the kitchen counter. I took the frame into the den, sat down at my computer, and did a Google image search. Five minutes later I was printing out a black-and-white photo of Elvis Presley in his army uniform. I inserted Elvis into the silver picture frame, gathered up the netting, and headed back to the shop.

For the next three hours I worked as fast and as hard as I'd ever worked before. I stapled and styled, draped and swagged and glue-gunned, until I was ready to drop. At four o'clock I forced myself to call it quits. The judges would be making their rounds at six, and I still had to assemble all the refreshments for the open house, and bathe and dress.

When I got out of the shower, I moaned at how little time I had left. My original plan had been to get myself up in some glam outfit from my collection of vintage clothes. Maybe a red chiffon cocktail dress from the sixties, with a gold lamé cinch belt. But there was no time now for primping and, anyway, glam wouldn't go with my theme.

Instead, I slicked my wild mane of red hair into a perky ponytail and caught it up with a big blue tulle bow. I pegged the hems of my blue jeans, rolling them calf-high, and slipped on a kitten-soft pale blue beaded cashmere sweater from my vintage collection that had been my Meemaw's. But Meemaw had never worn a push-up bra and left the top three pearl buttons undone like I did that night. Briefly I mourned again for the missing blue Christmas tree pin that had started this whole thing.

But I still had the old jewelry box the brooch had come from. I looped three different strands of the faux pearls around my neck and tripled another strand of pearls for a bracelet.

Bobby socks and saddle oxfords would have finished off my outfit, but I'd long ago tossed out the hated black-and-white shoes that had been a required part of our uniform at St. Vincent's Academy, the all-girl Catholic high school I'd attended. Instead, I slipped on a pair of black ballet flats, and as a last-minute thought, grabbed my daddy's old maroon Benedictine Catholic High School letter sweater.

I was heading back downstairs to start gathering up the

trays of food to take over to the shop when I heard a noise coming from the kitchen. I stopped abruptly on the last stair.

Footsteps, light but audible, were coming from the kitchen. I heard the sound of the heavy door of my Sub-Zero refrigerator door open and then close.

For a second, a chill ran down my spine. Somebody was in my house! Then I relaxed. Daniel. My prodigal boyfriend had come over to apologize for his uncaring attitude the night before.

"Daniel?" I called. "Are you on a mercy mission? Did you bring over the dessert trays you promised for the party?"

No answer. Quick footsteps, and then I heard the sound of the back door closing.

"Daniel?" I peeked around the door into the kitchen. It was empty, except for Jethro, who was crouched under the kitchen table, his tail thumping softly on the wooden floor.

I darted over to the back door just in time to see the wrought-iron garden gate swinging shut. I stepped outside to look. The only truck parked in my two-car carport was my own. The lane was empty.

Another chill ran down my spine. I walked quickly back to the kitchen, stepped inside, and locked the door behind me, throwing the latch on the dead bolt for good measure.

My hands were shaking, I realized. Jethro scooched forward on his belly and licked my bare ankle.

"Jethro," I scolded. "Why didn't you bark at the bad man?"

Thump thump went the tail.

I checked the refrigerator. Damn! The silver tray on which I'd carefully arranged five pounds of concentric circles of bacon-wrapped shrimp now held only a limp leaf of lettuce and a hollowed-out lemon half holding the cocktail sauce.

I ran into the dining room and pulled the drawer of my mahogany sideboard open. My grandmother's wedding silver, all eleven place settings of the Savannah pattern, were intact. My collection of sterling candlesticks on the dining room table was undisturbed.

In the living room, I picked up my purse from where I'd dropped it in the chair by the front door. My wallet was still stuffed with cash and credit cards. My checkbook was untouched.

I went back to the kitchen and picked up the phone and called Daniel's cell phone. I almost never disturb him when he's at the restaurant, especially this time of year, but this, I decided, was an emergency. I needed to be reassured by the sound of his voice.

"Weezie?" he said, answering after the second ring. "What's up?"

"Hi," I said, willing myself to stay calm. "Were you here just now?"

"No. Where? At your place? No. I'm asshole-deep in shrimp bisque here. Why?"

"Funny you should mention shrimp. Because mine are missing," I said, sinking down onto a kitchen chair. "Somebody was here," I said slowly. "In my kitchen. I'd just gotten dressed and I was coming downstairs when I heard somebody in the kitchen. I heard the refrigerator door being opened and closed. I just assumed it was you. But when I called your name, whoever it was left. I think I spooked him. They slipped out the back gate. With all my bacon-wrapped shrimp."

"Are you all right?"

"Fine," I said. "They left. That's all I care about."

"Was anything else taken? Did you call the cops?"

"No, I called you first," I said. "All my silver is still here. My purse was out in plain view. Nothing in it was touched, and I had the day's cash from the shop in my billfold, around five hundred bucks."

"Jesus!" he said. "How did they get in?"

"I don't know," I admitted, walking to the front of the house as I talked. "The front door still has the security latch on. Nobody got in that way." I walked back to the kitchen. "When I came in from the shop, I came in the back door. I've been running back and forth from the house to the shop all afternoon—"

"Well, did you lock the door the last time you came in?" he demanded.

"I can't remember," I wailed.

"Weezie!"

"I was in a big hurry," I said, near tears. "The judges are doing the historic district decorating contest at six, and I still needed to shower and dress, and get the food out for the open house—"

For the first time, I looked at the other silver trays of food I'd laid out on the kitchen counter, all neatly covered with plastic wrap. The platter of spinach-and-feta-stuffed mushrooms had been decimated. Likewise, the sausage cheese balls had been pillaged, and the mini crab quiches.

"Damn!" I cried. "They got the sausage balls. Not to mention the shrimp. Do you know how much I had to pay for jumbo shrimp?"

"Christ!" Daniel bellowed. "Forget the sausage balls and the judges. This is serious, Weezie. Somebody broke into your house while you were in the shower. You scared them off, otherwise. . . . Look, hang up and call the cops. Right now. I'm coming over there."

"No!" I shouted. "I'm fine. Nothing else was taken. Nobody was hurt. If you want to help me, send over something for me to feed this crowd of people I'm expecting. A cookie tray or something."

"I'm coming," Daniel insisted.

"No way," I said stubbornly. "You need to work. I need to work. Just . . . chill. Please? Okay? Maybe it was BeBe. In fact, I'm sure it was BeBe. She's supposed to come over and help me set up the food and bring her silver punch bowl for the Chatham Artillery Punch. It was BeBe, I'm positive. Which is probably why Jethro didn't bark."

"Jethro didn't bark? Somebody came in your house and he didn't bark?"

"Not a yip," I said, leaning down to scratch Jethro's ears.

"He still barks his head off when I come in the door," Daniel said darkly.

"That's different. You're a man. He thinks he's defending my honor."

"Well . . . lock the door."

"I did. I will."

"Promise me you won't forget again," he said. "There's bad guys running around downtown, Weezie. I had a customer robbed at gunpoint yesterday just after he left the restaurant at midnight."

"I'll be careful," I promised.

"Good," he said, his voice softening. "So, Jethro came home last night?"

"Yeah," I said. "That's another strange story. In fact, a lot of strange stuff has been happening around here the last couple days."

"You can tell me tonight," he said. "I'm staying over. And I'll send one of the busboys over with some appetizers and a cookie tray for your party. Okay?"

"That would be great," I said.

"Good luck with the decorating contest," Daniel said. "Knock 'em dead, kid."

CHAPTER 8

After I hung up the phone I got down on all fours and went eyeball to eyeball with my little furry buddy. "Did you eat up all my expensive appetizers, Jethro? Did you, Ro-Ro?"

Thump thump went the tail. He was the sweetest, most loyal dog God had ever created, but he was also, alas, one of the dumbest. Anyway, he was in the clear, since his breath smelled like Kibbles 'n Bits, not garlic and shrimp.

"Yoo-hoo!" BeBe was banging on the back door. I went over and unlocked it, and she struggled in under the weight of a heavy silver punch bowl, on top of which rested a huge white cardboard box.

"I've brought pecan tassies and chocolate chewies from Gottlieb's Bakery," she said, setting the boxes on the counter. "I figure if you can't win the decorating contest fair and square, we'll just bribe the judges with these little goodies."

"Thanks for the vote of confidence," I told her. "Were you just here a few minutes ago?"

"No," she said, looking puzzled. "I stopped at Gottlieb's first, and I just now drove up around back. Why?"

"Somebody was here," I said grimly. "Right here in this kitchen, while I was upstairs getting showered and dressed. I heard footsteps, and the refrigerator door opening and closing. I called down, thinking it was Daniel, and whoever it was took off out the back door."

"Good Lord," BeBe said, clutching her purse. "Burglars! Did you check your jewelry?"

"I'm wearing the only good jewelry I own," I said, gesturing at the diamond stud earrings that had been a birthday gift from Daniel. "Relax. All they got was the sausage balls." I gestured toward the half-empty party platters. "And the stuffed mushrooms and the bacon-wrapped shrimp."

"Not the shrimp," BeBe moaned. "They're my absolute favorites. I've been thinking of those shrimp all afternoon."

"You'll get over it," I said. I transferred the contents of one half-empty platter to another and rearranged the garnish and the plastic wrap. "Come on. We've got to start getting set up at the shop. The judges will be here in half an hour."

BeBe picked up the punch bowl and the cookie box and followed me out the door, giving a backward glance at Jethro. "You're sure your burglar wasn't the four-footed kind?"

"Positive," I said, locking the door behind us. "Jethro can't open the refrigerator. Or the back door. And I distinctly heard somebody do both."

"Oh," she said, following me over to the shop's back door. "Did you call the cops?"

"To report a case of purloined sausage balls? I somehow think the Savannah police have higher-priority cases than that these days."

"Spooky," BeBe said, stepping aside to let me unlock the door, which, I noted with satisfaction, was securely locked.

"You don't know the half of it," I said, stepping inside. "All kinds of creepy stuff has been happening around here."

But BeBe hadn't stopped to hear my story. She'd put her contribution to the party down on the big pine table at the back of Maisie's Daisy, and gone straight outside. I could see her, standing outside on the sidewalk, staring rapturously in at the window.

I smiled and switched on all the shop lights. The forest of aluminum trees lit up, and the thousands of tiny white lights I'd wrapped the shop's walls and ceilings with, hidden behind the mists of blue tulle, shone like little stars in a darkened sky. On the shelf above the cash register, I punched a button, and the shop's sound system started playing the special Christmas compilation CD I'd burned earlier in the day, after downloading my favorite oldies off the Internet. Brenda Lee's "Rocking Around the Christmas Tree" wafted through the store and out to the sidewalk, courtesy of the mini speakers Daniel had mounted on brackets over the shop's front door.

"It's perfect," BeBe said, when I joined her outside on the sidewalk. "Oh, Weezie, it's like a little movie set."

She glanced over at me and laughed. "Now I get why you're dressed like Rizzo from *Grease*."

"Not Rizzo," I corrected her, adjusting my pearls. "More like Sandra Dee."

"Whatever," she said, turning back to the window. "If those

judges don't give you first place, I'll have 'em impeached. I'll demand a recount."

All modesty aside, the window *was* divine.

I'd set two of the aluminum trees on either side of the front door of the shop, decked out in the cheap blue and silver glass balls and big blue lights. I'd spray-painted the previously rejected grapevines with flat white paint, draped them with more of the blue tulle, and wrapped them with white twinkle lights. And the color wheel I'd hidden at the base of each tree bathed the front of the shop in a deep blue light.

From inside the window, the halo effect of all that gauzy blue tulle artfully bunched in soft drifts gave the whole scene a dreamlike quality.

"It reminds me of one of those little dioramas we used to make in shoe boxes for school book reports," BeBe said. "But this one's called Blue Christmas, right?"

"So you get it?" I asked, delighted.

"How could I not?"

Inside the window, the blue lights on the aluminum trees had an almost eerie effect. On the other side of the window, I'd styled a fantasy fifties teenage girl's bedroom, complete with the silver-framed picture of Elvis on the nightstand. Beside Elvis, I'd placed an old-timey glass Coke bottle with a straw sticking out the top, and beside that was a paper plate with a slice of pizza, all of it illuminated by a kitschy formerly pink poodle lamp I'd mercilessly given the blue paint treatment to.

The blue princess phone was in the middle of the bed, waiting for that call from that special boy. Beside the phone

I'd propped up my own much-loved childhood teddy bear. His little black shoe-button eyes gleamed with some sort of secret amusement. And beside Teddy, I'd placed an open diary with a feather-tipped pen.

"Perfect," BeBe said, nudging me. "You should go in and lie on the bed and pretend to be a mannequin."

"That reminds me," I said, darting back inside the shop. I tiptoed into the vignette and took off the heavy gold Savannah High class ring that had been a gift from a long-forgotten boyfriend, and set the ring on the page of the open diary. Then I lovingly draped my daddy's letter sweater across the foot of the bed.

I heard a pair of hands clapping and, looking up, saw BeBe outside, where she'd been joined by a small knot of bystanders. One by one, they started clapping too, until I realized I was being given a standing ovation.

Modestly, I bowed low, and when I straightened up, I saw Judy McConnell, the president of the downtown business association, pinning a First Place ribbon to the wreath on the door. Appropriately enough, it was blue.

CHAPTER 9

The punch," I cried, suddenly jolted back into my role as shopkeeper and hostess. "We can't have a Christmas open house without the punch!"

I first tasted Chatham Artillery Punch as a fourteen-year-old kid, when I snuck a cup of it at a family wedding and spent the rest of the evening passed out under the piano at the Knights of Columbus hall. My mother, certain that I'd been abducted and sold into white slavery, was on the verge of calling the cops, when my cousin Butch found me curled up underneath the Steinway.

Chatham Artillery Punch isn't something you pour out of a couple of cans of fruit juice and call it a day. No, sir. The recipe I've always used, which is my adaptation of the one in the Savannah Junior League cookbook, the one with the great Ogden Nash limerick in the front, suggests that the hostess start the base of the punch at least two months ahead of time, preferably making it in a forty-gallon drum.

I hadn't started two months ahead of time, nor did I have any empty forty-gallon drums at my disposal.

Instead I'd mixed up my batch the previous week in a brand-new galvanized tin trash can, bought especially for this purpose.

My recipe calls for the following:

2 liters of rum

1 liter of gin

1 liter of bourbon

1 liter of brandy

3 bottles of rosé wine

¼ pound of green tea steeped in two quarts of boiling water

2 ½ cups of light brown sugar, dissolved in the hot tea

2 cups of maraschino cherries

2 large cans of chunked pineapple in their juice

Juice of 9 lemons

The original, classic recipe also calls for a pinch of gunpowder for that final, explosive charge, but I'd decided my version was explosive enough without the gunpowder.

I'd made the base, covered it with the lid, which I'd tightened with a bungee cord, and stashed it out on my patio all week, where the cool weather kept it nicely. After five days, I'd siphoned the punch off into washed and emptied plastic gallon milk jugs.

"Jeez," BeBe said, holding the punch bowl steady while I poured in my brew, "This stuff smells like a whole distillery. What's the alcohol content, do you think?"

"Lethal," I assured her. I went back into the stockroom, to the freezer compartment of the shop's refrigerator, and retrieved the cherry-and-lemon-encrusted ice ring I'd stashed there the day before.

Once the ice ring was floating in the bowl, I added the finishing touch, a bottle of champagne.

I filled two cups with the punch, handed one to BeBe, and kept the other for myself. BeBe clicked her cup against the side of mine. "To the victors go the spoils," she declared.

"Yowza!" she said after her initial sip. "I haven't really drunk any of this stuff since my debutante ball."

"What happened that night?" I asked.

"No idea." She grinned. "I shotgunned a couple snorts of the stuff, and when I woke up the next day, I'd taken a road trip to Jacksonville with the bass player from the rock band Mama'd hired for the party. She made me have the tattoo removed too."

"Take it slow," I advised, blinking at the depth charge from my own sip. "I'm counting on you staying sober back here at the refreshments, while I mind the store."

As soon as I unlocked the front door and announced the open house was officially open, people began to stream inside.

Judy McConnell was the first one in the door. "You know you broke all the contest rules, right?"

"Silly little rules," I said. "And yet you gave me first prize anyway."

"I want that aluminum tree in the window," she said, taking out her checkbook. "How much?"

I shook my head. "Sorry. It's not for sale. All the stuff in the window is from my personal collection."

She cocked her head and gave me a winning smile. "And yet we gave you first prize."

"Ninety bucks," I said quickly. "But you can't pick it up until Saturday. And if you tell anybody about this, I'll have to kill you."

"Deal," she said. "We would have given you first prize anyway. Your window rocks. Way more original than anything else we've seen in years."

I couldn't resist. "What about Babalu? The snow queens didn't grab you this year?"

"Having the children's choir from Turner A.M.E. Church dressed up in white robes singing 'Walkin' in a Winter Wonderland' was too over the top. Even for me," Judy said, wrinkling her nose. "And we lost a judge who slipped on that awful artificial snow they're blowing and wrenched her ankle."

Within a matter of minutes, Maisy's Daisy was full to capacity. The music played, and the punch got drunk, and people seemed to be in a very merry, non-blue mood. I saw lots of our regular customers, like Steve the banker, who stops by the shop every Wednesday afternoon. He's bought every old oscillating fan and Bakelite radio I've ever had. Tacky Jacky, my upholsterer client, came in too, and left with an armload of the vintage barkcloth drapes and cutter quilts she buys to make the designer throw pillows we sell in the shop.

But lots of the other customers were tourists, drawn in by

the irresistible music that spilled out onto the sidewalk, and of course, by our prizewinning decorations.

While BeBe doled out the punch and kept the appetizer platters refilled, I manned the cash register, which jingled merrily with all the purchases people were making. Our customers seemed to be grabbing up and buying everything that wasn't nailed down. And so many people kept trying to dismantle the display window to buy stuff, I finally had to scrawl a big sign on the back of a paper sack that said "Sorry! Window Display Is from Owner's Personal Collection—Not for Sale!"

By ten o'clock, an hour past our posted nine o'clock closing time, I finally had to physically escort Steve the banker out the front door. He had two huge shopping bags full of merchandise in each hand, but he wasn't done yet.

"But, I've really got to have the blue princess phone from the window," Steve was saying. "It's the perfect thing for the beach house at Tybee. It'll be a Christmas present for Polly."

"Not for sale, Steve," I said firmly.

He pressed his face to the glass. "Not even for Polly?"

His wife, Polly, was an old friend from high school days.

"All right." I sighed, giving in. "Thirty bucks. But you can't pick it up until Saturday. And if you tell anybody I sold you anything from that window, I'll have to kill you."

"Deal," he said, grinning ear to ear. "And what about the turntable?"

"Don't push your luck." I pulled down the window shade to end the discussion.

CHAPTER 10

Daniel arrived at the town house just in time to help wash up the last of the empty platters from the party and to play the role of chef and waiter to BeBe and me, serving up steaming bowls of sherry-laced she-crab soup to us in front of the fireplace in the living room while we conducted our usual party postmortem.

"I'm whipped," I announced, pushing my bowl away. "I want to go to bed and sleep for a year."

Daniel shoved me over on the sofa and plopped down beside me. "The bed part I can arrange. The year's worth of sleep I can't guarantee."

"Did you notice the shop's display window?" I asked, putting my feet in his lap.

He took the hint and started massaging my calves.

"It looked great," he said. "Congratulations on winning. It was kinda unusual though, huh?"

"Originality," I said. "It's all about originality. And I have you to thank for the idea."

"How's that?" he asked.

"You and your Christmas funk," I said lightly, deliberately avoiding the cause of his holiday moodiness. "Blue Christmas. It made me think of the Elvis song, and then, I just kinda spun it into this whole story line about a teenage girl missing her boyfriend at Christmas."

"I think I saw a photographer from the newspaper taking pictures tonight," BeBe volunteered. "You're gonna be famous."

"And I promise not to forget the little people I stepped on along the way," I said. Daniel gave my toes a playful squeeze.

"Anyway, it was a great party," BeBe said, mopping up the last of the soup with a chunk of French bread. She wriggled her sock-clad toes on the ottoman in front of her chair. "Daniel, you saved the day with that food you sent over."

"Just so you let everybody know it came from Guale," Daniel said. "I'm all about promotion, now that I own the joint."

"I was handing out the menus to everybody who came near the food table," BeBe promised. "And everybody just inhaled your crab dip and the deviled oysters. I've never seen so much food disappear so fast."

"And merchandise," I said gleefully. "I think I had my biggest day in the history of the shop tonight."

"How big?" BeBe asked.

"Big enough that I can afford to forget about that twenty-five-hundred-dollar table you sold for two fifty yesterday."

She stuck her tongue out at me, and I returned the favor.

"I didn't even get any of the desserts you brought, BeBe," I said. "They were all gone by the time I made my way through the crowd to the food table."

"They were a hit, no doubt about it," BeBe said. "I almost forgot to tell you. I saw one woman filling up her tote bag with the pecan tassies and chocolate chewies."

"One of my customers?" I asked, indignant. "Why didn't you say something about it to me?"

"You were busy. And I didn't want to make a federal case out of it. Anyway, I doubt she was one of your regulars."

"Are you sure she didn't slip anything else in her purse? Something more valuable than some cookies?" Daniel asked. "You know, Weezie scared off a burglar here earlier today."

"I kept my eye on the woman the rest of the night," BeBe said. "She knocked back a lot of that punch though. I don't know how she could even stand up, let alone walk, with as much as she drank. But she seemed fine. She mostly just walked around and around the shop, smiling and taking it all in."

"What did she look like?" I asked.

BeBe scrunched up her face in concentration. "Nothing special or out of the ordinary. Maybe mid-sixties. Short salt-and-pepper hair that was kind of wavy. Her clothes weren't what you'd call stylish. She was wearing like a brown sweater, and baggy, sort of blue wool slacks. And instead of a real pocketbook, she had one of those canvas tote bags, like they give you at bookstores sometimes. Oh yeah, I thought this was cute. She was wearing this little blue Christmas tree pin on her sweater. I noticed it, because it fit in so well with the theme of your window, Weezie."

Daniel sat up straight on the sofa, and we exchanged startled glances.

" A blue Christmas tree pin?" I asked. "That's too much of a coincidence. It's got to be my pin. Damn! She must be the one who stole it out of my truck."

"What are you talking about?" Daniel demanded. "You never told me somebody broke into your truck. When did this happen?"

"Last night," I said. "After I got back from James and Jonathan 's party and went searching for Jethro."

"You should have called me," Daniel said. "I would have come right back. This is serious, Weezie. Your truck first, and then your house. I want you to call the cops right now and have them come over and fill out a police report."

"I'm not even sure the truck was broken into," I protested. "And I didn't tell you because I haven't had time. But I'm telling you now."

"What happened?" BeBe asked. "I still don't get when all this took place."

I took a deep breath. "It started last night, after Daniel dropped me off here. We'd had a fight—"

"It wasn't really a fight," Daniel interrupted. "You were pissed because I had to go back to work. You don't seem to understand how busy the holidays are at a restaurant."

"Maybe it wasn't a full-fledged fight, but I was definitely still pissed at you," I said evenly. "I do realize how busy you are at work, but I really wish you weren't such a cranky old bastard around the holidays. You know how much I love Christmas."

"Hey!" BeBe called, holding up her hands in a defensive gesture. "This isn't supposed to be couples counseling here. Just tell me about these weird break-ins."

"I know you love Christmas," Daniel said. "But I can't help it if I don't. And I think you could be a little more understanding about the reasons why I'm not exactly all into the whole damned jolly holly-day deal."

"The break-ins," BeBe repeated. "Just stick to the facts, ma'am."

"Okay," I said, taking a deep breath. "When I got back here last night, Jethro took off out the front door. I drove around downtown, for hours, looking for him, but he'd just disappeared. I was heartsick. I slept on the sofa, so that if he came home, I'd hear him at the door and let him in. But he stayed out all night. He's never done anything like that before."

"Boys will be boys. Maybe he has a lady friend," BeBe suggested.

"Maybe," I said dubiously. "This morning, when I went out to get the paper, I looked up, and there was Jethro, inside my truck!"

"How'd he get in the truck?" BeBe asked.

"Somebody had to have put him there," I said. "There was a little piece of old string tied to his collar, and they'd loosely tied the other end to the steering wheel. And the windows were cranked down a little, so he'd have enough air." I gave Daniel a defiant look. "I know I didn't leave those windows rolled down. It was cold last night. I even had the heater on."

"I believe you," Daniel said apologetically. "Go on."

"Jethro was fine. There wasn't a scratch on him," I said. "And I didn't realize until later on today that something was missing from my truck."

"The blue Christmas tree pin," BeBe suggested.

"I wore it to the Christmas party," I said. "Pinned to my black velvet shawl. But I left my shawl in the truck overnight," I said. "And it was right there, where I left it, when I found Jethro the next morning. He'd used it as a bed. But the pin was gone."

"What else?" Daniel asked. "Was anything else taken?"

"Not a thing," I said. "Nothing else was touched, as far as I know."

"You've got to be more careful about locking up," Daniel began. "The crime rate downtown—"

"Don't start," I warned. "I usually do lock the truck. And the house. It's like somebody was watching, waiting for the opportunity to break in, the one time my life is especially hectic, and I let down my guard."

"Was the pin especially valuable?" BeBe asked.

"No," I said. "Like I told Daniel, hundreds of thousands of those pins were made by dozens of manufacturers from the forties through the sixties. The pin I bought in the box lot at the auction was nicely made, but it was definitely costume jewelry. I could go on eBay right now and buy another one just like it, probably for under fifty bucks."

"Maybe you just think it's junk jewelry," BeBe said, starting to warm up to her theory. "Maybe the pin was made of real sapphires. And gold. And the person who stole it knew what it was worth. Maybe they tried to buy it at the auction, and when you got it instead, they decided to follow you home and steal it from you."

"Back away from the Nancy Drew mysteries, BeBe," I suggested. "I bought three boxes of stuff at that auction in Hardeeville, for which I paid a grand total of seven dollars. The only other bidder was a redheaded lady named Estelle, who wasn't willing to pay more than five bucks, which is how I ended up with the winning bid."

"Oh," BeBe said.

"Although," I said slowly. "I think somebody else did follow me over to Hardeeville yesterday."

"Who?" BeBe demanded.

"Manny Alvarez."

"Who?" Daniel asked.

"One of the guys who own Babalu, the shop across the square. He just showed up at the auction, out of nowhere. None of the other Savannah dealers go over there, except me. It's like my secret source. But that day, Manny showed up. He outbid me for this great old Sunbeam bread display rack," I groused. "You should have seen the damn smug expression on his face. I could have throttled him when he hit two hundred dollars."

"Maybe Manny Alvarez broke into your truck," BeBe exclaimed. "Maybe he was just as pissed about you winning as you were at him."

"Impossible," I said, shaking my head. "He wasn't there when I bought the box lots. He left as soon as he paid for the bread rack. And, anyway, he wouldn't have known the Christmas tree pin was there. It was in a jewelry case in the bottom of the last cardboard box. Trader Bob didn't even know what all was in those boxes. I bought everything pretty much sight unseen."

"Maybe he was skulking around outside, waiting for you to leave," BeBe said, persisting in her conspiracy theory.

"Why would this very successful, independently wealthy antiques dealer break into my truck and take only a silly, kitschy little pin?" I asked. "And for that matter, why would he walk into my kitchen—knowing I'm home, and steal my appetizers? Why?"

"Sabotage," BeBe said darkly. "He wanted to sabotage your open house. He's jealous of all your success. He can't stand it that you out-decorated him. I mean, he's a gay guy. Nobody out-decorates gay guys."

I yawned and stood up. "You're crazy. And I'm tired." I pulled Daniel to his feet.

"Bedtime," I said meaningfully.

CHAPTER 11

Daniel's breathing was as steady and reassuring as the ticking of the Baby Ben alarm clock on my nightstand. So why wasn't I asleep too? God knows, I was tired. And I had fallen fast asleep after a gentle, lazy session of lovemaking. Now I propped myself up on one elbow and examined Daniel's face in the moonlight streaming through the bedroom's lace curtains.

His dark, wavy hair needed cutting again, and although I knew he shaved every night before going on duty at Guale, his five o'clock shadow was already in evidence. His skin, still tanned from a summer and fall of fishing, crabbing, and working on his cottage at Tybee Island, shone dark against the bleached white cotton sheets. A study in black and white. Light and dark. Why, I kept wondering, was his soul so dark at this time of year? And what, if anything, could I do to change him?

I heard a light scratching at the bedroom door and sat up, as Jethro pushed the bedroom door open with his nose.

"You too?" I asked, getting out of bed and following him downstairs. We went through the kitchen, and I unlocked the back door and let him outside, shivering in the blast of cold air that met me.

Jethro barked a short, happy bark, and when I looked out, he was gone. The garden gate was swinging in the wind.

"Damn." I moaned. I'd checked and double-checked that all the doors were locked after BeBe had gone home and before we'd gone to bed. But I'd forgotten to remind BeBe to make sure the gate latched securely behind her when she went to get her car.

I shoved my feet into a pair of beat-up loafers I keep by the back door for gardening, and ran out through the garden to the lane. It was empty.

"Damn," I repeated. Upstairs, I threw on a pair of flannel pajama bottoms and the sweater Daniel had worn earlier in the evening. But he was sleeping so soundly, I didn't have the heart to wake him.

Just as I'd done the night before, I trolled the squares around Charlton Street in my truck, softly calling Jethro's name out the window, searching in the dark for my prodigal puppy.

An hour later, I'd spotted dozens of cats, one terrified-looking 'possum, and half a dozen homeless men and women stretched out on park benches and in the bushes in the squares, but no black-and-white mutt.

I drove home and parked the truck at the curb in front of

the town house, being careful to leave the truck's doors unlocked. Maybe Jethro's guardian angel would find him and bring him home again. Maybe he'd even leave behind my blue Chrismas tree pin. And maybe, I thought ruefully, if pigs had wings they wouldn't bump their butts when they tried to fly.

Sleep came quickly this time around, and when my doorbell started buzzing noisily a few hours later, I had no idea what time it was, or where I was.

Still in Daniel's sweater and the plaid pajama bottoms, I stumbled downstairs and opened the door.

"Jethro!" I exclaimed.

He was sitting on his haunches, looking up expectantly, almost like he was peddling hairbrushes door-to-door and had finally reached a cooperative housewife.

"Eloise!" Standing slightly to the right of Jethro, looking extremely peeved, was my neighbor and sworn enemy, Cookie Parker.

I glanced at my watch. It was barely eight o'clock, but Cookie was dressed in immaculate black wool slacks and an enormous Burberry plaid sweater. A matching plaid tam-o'-shanter was perched on his pumpkin-size pate.

"You found Jethro," I said, grabbing both his hands and shaking them. "Thank you so much for bringing him home."

"I found him, all right," Cookie said coolly. "He was assaulting my Ruthie!"

I rubbed the sleep out of my eyes and yawned.

"Assaulting?"

Cookie blushed. "You know what I mean."

"No," I assured him. "I don't. You mean they were fighting?" I knelt down and took a closer look to assess Jethro's wounds. But I didn't see any.

"He was humping her, all right?" Cookie blurted. "Is that crude enough for you?"

"Jethro?"

Noncommittal, he licked his privates. Jethro, that is. Cookie just stood there, quivering with rage and indignation.

I stood up and yawned again. "Well, what do you want me to do about it? I mean, I'm sorry, okay? I got up around one this morning, to let him outside, and I guess my friend forgot to latch the garden gate. We had a pretty busy, late night last night."

Cookie pursed his lips. "We were well aware of your enchanted evening. I suppose congratulations are in order." He thrust out his hand and shook mine limply.

"Thank you," I said.

"It was an amusing display, I'll give you that," Cookie allowed. "Manny and I were just saying last night that the judges must have decided to go with camp this year, rather than beauty or artistic vision."

I supposed this was his version of a compliment. I decided to accept it, but then I had the impulse to giggle, which I managed to stifle.

"I thought Babalu looked beautiful, from what I saw of it," I said.

He shrugged. "It wasn't that big a deal to me. But Manny! The poor dear was devastated. He really puts his whole heart into these little competitions. He's been planning this winter wonderland tableau since July."

It was cold. Really cold. I looked down. My toes were turning blue. I edged them up under Jethro's butt, grateful for the borrowed warmth.

"Well," I said, anxious to go inside and back to bed. "Better luck next time. And I really am sorry about Jethro's, um, lapse in judgment. I don't know what's gotten into him lately. This is the second time in a week he's run away like this."

Cookie bit his lip. "I just hope Ruthie's not . . . well . . . you know."

"Not what?"

"Enceinte," he said, blushing violently. "This is only the second time she's come into . . ." He blushed again and stared at something above my head. "You know."

I blinked. "Oh. Wait. You mean your bitch is in heat? Oh, no."

"Yes," he said quietly. "Exactly."

I prodded Jethro with my bare foot. "Bad boy!"

He thumped his tail in perfect agreement.

"Wait," I said slowly. "If your dog was in heat, what was she doing out?"

"She never goes outside without one of us. Ruthie has two *very* protective papas. But last night, after the judges left and we found out *you'd* won the decorating contest, well, Manny was so distraught, I had to do something to take his mind off our rather crushing disappointment. We were supposed to have our open house last night too. But we just couldn't put on our happy party faces. I called the caterer and told her to come and take all the food to the children's home. Then I took Manny over to the Pink House for a quiet, intimate fireside dinner. Long story short, our garden gate got left unlatched too last night. Although I don't quite understand how or when. Manny got up sometime in the night to let Ruthie out, and then just stumbled back to bed without checking on her again."

His lips pursed. "Let me tell you, Mister Macho won't be making a mistake like that again anytime soon. Ruthie could have been dognapped."

Cookie sighed. "Latin men! You love them because of their fiery, passionate lust for life. But you forget, or at least I do, that the downside to all that passion is a darker, deeper despair than most Anglo men feel."

All this, I thought, over a decorating contest.

"As a result," Cookie continued, "Manny, I'm afraid, got absolutely *trashed* on mojitos."

My lips were twitching again. To cover, I yawned.

"And then he acted out," Cookie said, lowering his voice.

"How?"

"He stripped down to his Tommies and went skinny-dipping in that fountain in the middle of Lafayette Square!" Cookie said. "Can you imagine—if the bishop had looked out his window and seen something like that?"

Living as he did in the historic district, I felt fairly sure that the bishop at Cathedral of St. John the Baptist, which fronted Lafayette Square, had probably seen worse. But I kept that to myself.

"No," I said sympathetically.

"It was not an attractive display," Cookie said. "When I finally hauled him out of there, he insisted on coming over here. To your place. I think he was somehow planning to vandalize your window. As revenge."

Alarmed, I stepped out of the house to see what, if anything had happened to my shop.

"Not to worry," Cookie said. "I managed to drag him away before he did any harm."

"I'm glad of that," I said.

"Although," he went on, "I'm afraid Manny did manage to wake up your employee. She looked pretty startled, and who can blame her? A dripping-wet, half-naked gorgeous Cuban man brandishing a can of spray paint at two in the morning."

"Employee?" I was drawing a blank.

"Or maybe one of your customers or party guests got overserved and decided it was safer to stay right where she was."

"Cookie," I said finally. "What are you talking about?"

"I'm talking about the woman who was sleeping in that bed in your shop window last night," he said. "Tucked in tight, teddy bear and all."

CHAPTER 12

I pulled the collar of Daniel's sweater tighter around my neck, to ward off the sudden chill.

"Is—" I gulped. "Is she still there?"

"I don't know," Cookie snapped. "I cut through the square to get to your place, so he"—he glared down at Jethro—"could stop and do his business there, instead of on my doorstep."

He thrust a plastic Kroger bag at me. "This is for you."

It was still warm. I held it at arm's length. "Thanks. And, again, I'm sorry about Jethro's bad behavior."

"Sorry just doesn't cut it," Cookie said, his nostrils flaring in anger. "You should have had that dog fixed. There are enough mutts running around loose downtown—"

"Look," I said angrily, shoving Jethro inside my door, "we'll have to continue this discussion some other time. If there's somebody sleeping in my window, I need to get over to the shop and see about it."

"I should hope so," Cookie said, and he turned and flounced off, his tam-o'-shanter bouncing with every step.

After depositing Jethro's poop in the kitchen trash can, I took the stairs two at a time, calling out as I went.

"Daniel! Wake up! One of the neighbors says he saw somebody sleeping in the bed at Maisie's Daisy."

No answer. Daniel is such a sound sleeper, he could—and has—slept through a hurricane.

"Daniel!" I yanked the blanket and sheet off the bed, and shook his bare shoulder repeatedly. "Wake up!"

"What?" He rolled onto his stomach and buried his head under the pillows.

"You've got to come over to the shop with me," I said, stepping out of the pajama bottoms and pulling on a pair of jeans. "That was Cookie Parker at the door just now. He says he saw a woman sleeping in the display window in the shop earlier this morning."

"Why?" Daniel swung his legs over the side of the bed. I tossed his jeans at him.

"Come on. Hurry up and get dressed. I'm not going over there by myself."

"Crazy," Daniel muttered, but a minute later he was right behind me on the stairs. When we got to the front door, he reached out and grabbed my hand.

"You better stay here," he said quietly. "If this is the same person who broke into your truck, and then the house, there's no telling how crazy she is. Just stay here. Call the cops."

"What? No cops. I'm coming with you," I insisted.

He put both hands on my shoulders. "Please? Just this once, listen to me?"

I shook my head. "It's probably just a harmless little old lady. The same one BeBe saw snitching cookies last night. We can't call the cops on her. They'll lock her up in jail. I don't want that on my conscience. Not at Christmas."

"Christmas again!" But he stood aside to let me out the door.

"Not all these homeless people downtown are the quaint little hoboes you seem to visualize," he said. "There're a couple of guys who were coming around the back door at the restaurant at closing time, mooching food. The busboys felt sorry for them, were giving them some of the leftovers we donate to the food bank. But a couple of nights ago, one of them started demanding money. He actually threatened Kevin with a knife."

"Lock the door," I said over my shoulder, already down the front steps of the town house. "I know you're worried about my safety, and I appreciate it. But this isn't some knife-wielding psycho. Cookie said it was a woman. And she was asleep—clutching my teddy bear."

"Probably had a revolver under the pillow," he said darkly when he caught up with me on the sidewalk outside the shop.

"She's gone." I was surprised at how let down I felt, staring in at the display window.

"Thank God," he said.

We both stood there, staring at my vision of a Blue Christmas.

"It's just like I left it," I said. And it was, mostly. The chenille spread was smooth, the pillows were arranged just as I'd placed them the night before. The feather pen was still poised atop the open diary. The class ring was still there. The blue princess phone, the poodle lamp, even the records were fanned out in the same order around the phonograph. Elvis's upper lip still curled up at me from the silver-framed picture.

"We'd better go inside and see what's missing," Daniel said. "And I don't care if they do have to lock somebody up, if anything's been stolen, we are calling the cops."

"Okay," I said meekly, knowing that a call wouldn't be necessary.

Daniel followed me inside, walking every inch of the shop, peering inside cupboards, checking the bathroom, he even got down on his hands and knees and looked under the bed, until he was satisfied that it was empty.

"This Cookie guy, was he sure he saw somebody in *your* shop?" he asked, yawning. "I mean, is there any chance he was mistaken?"

"Well, he admitted he and Manny had been drinking," I said. "Actually, he said Manny was so upset at losing the decorating contest that he got shit-faced last night over cocktails at the Pink House."

"The Pink House!" Daniel's eyes narrowed.

I knew immediately it had been a mistake to mention Guale's closest restaurant competition downtown.

"Anyway," I added hastily, "Manny got so trashed he stripped down to his skivvies and went for a dip in the Lafayette Square fountain. And then he came over here, apparently to spray-paint graffiti on my windows. Fortunately, Cookie got him calmed down and put a stop to it. But that's when they both saw the woman asleep in my display bed."

Daniel yawned again.

"She's gone now, that's for sure. *If* she ever really was here. I know the bartender at the Pink House. She makes drinks strong enough to stop a bull moose in his tracks. I think she thinks it helps her tips."

I nodded thoughtfully, following Daniel out the front door and stopping to lock up. But he was already in front of the town house, standing on my front stoop.

"I'll make us breakfast," he offered. "French toast. You've got eggs and milk, right?"

"Yeah," I called back, looking in at the shop window again. My gaze lingered on the iron bed's footboard, where my father's high school letter sweater had hung the night before. The sweater was gone, and in its place was a threadbare brown sweater with a glittery blue Christmas tree brooch pinned to the collar.

CHAPTER 13

Three days before Christmas, and I still hadn't finished my shopping. Still, when BeBe offered to feed me dinner if I'd come over and help her wrap her gifts, along with my own, it was an offer I couldn't refuse.

BeBe is strictly a wrapping paper-and-ribbon girl, while I have always been one of those demented souls who insist on making every gift a perfect little work of art. Which meant that by ten o'clock that night, we'd drunk two bottles of wine, finished dinner and dessert, and wrapped all her gifts, while I was still slaving away over mine.

I was hot-gluing a string of fake pearls to a glossy black box to which I'd already affixed a vintage scrap of lace collar when BeBe came back into the study of her town house with another glass of wine.

"That looks amazing," she said. "Who's it for?"

As an answer, I opened the box and held up the contents.

BeBe winced. "The dreaded seasonal sweater. For your mother, right?"

"I know," I said. "But she just loves these things. And Valentine's Day is the only holiday she doesn't already have a sweater for. So . . ."

She scratched a fingernail against the appliquéd calico hearts on the pocket of the hot pink cardigan, then pointed at the white satin cupid shooting an embroidered arrow across the sweater's chest.

"Eloise," BeBe said sternly, "this is the most atrocious garment I have ever seen. Where in God's name did you buy the thing?"

"The Internet, natch."

"What's the site called, TackyTogs dot com?"

"Worse," I said, laughing. "The Kitten's Whiskers."

She put the top back on the box and pushed it away in distaste.

"I know you bought your dad another power tool, and I saw those beautiful leather books you wrapped up for James and Jonathan, but what did you buy for Daniel?"

I put the glue gun down and flopped onto my back on BeBe's Oriental carpet.

"Nothing," I wailed. "You know he's always hated Christmas. And it's worse than ever this year. He says he doesn't need anything, and he doesn't want me to buy him anything at all. It's so Grinch-y. But he's absolutely adamant about it."

"Ridiculous," BeBe said. "It's just a typical male ploy to get out of buying *you* a good present. Like an engagement ring," she said meaningfully.

"No," I said quickly. "I really believe he means what he says. You know he buys me wonderful birthday gifts, and even silly little no-special-occasion gifts. So I know it's not that. Besides, I don't want a ring. Not for Christmas, anyway."

"It's that whole weird family thing of his, isn't it?" BeBe asked.

She was intimately acquainted with Daniel's family saga, since it was she who'd uncovered the whole sad story back when Daniel was still working for her at Guale.

"Yeah," I said glumly. "His father left at Christmas. His brothers still live here in town, but Eric and Derek are busy with their own lives, and for Daniel, the restaurant just seems to eat up all his free time."

"Don't I know it," BeBe said. "That's one reason I finally decided to let Guale go. I wanted a chance at having a real life with Harry."

BeBe had inherited Harry Sorrentino, along with a broken-down mom-and-pop motel out on Tybee Island, less than a year ago, through an unfortunate encounter with a gorgeous con man who ultimately fleeced her. But, in typical BeBe fashion, she'd managed to track the guy down, get her money back, and keep and refurbish the inn into a money-making proposition.

Unquestionably, Harry, the only charter boat captain I know who reads Wodehouse and John D. MacDonald, was the best part of that particular acquisition.

"Speaking of which," I said. "What are you giving Harry? I know we wrapped a bunch of boxes."

She giggled and blushed. "Harry is the world's easiest lay.

He likes everything. So I went a little nuts, even though it is our first Christmas together. Let's see. Of course, there's that Hawaiian shirt you bought him at that yard sale down in Florida."

"For two bucks," I reminded her.

"Right. Harry loves a bargain as much as you, so I left the price tag on it. Oh yeah. I got him a fancy Shimano reel, and a new pair of Top-Siders to wear when he's out on the *Jitterbug*, and this one's my favorite: I commissioned a portrait of Jeeves."

"BeBe!" I exclaimed. "That's a great idea."

Jeeves, Harry's Yorkshire terrier, was like Harry's child, and although BeBe always professed to hate dogs, I knew she secretly adored the little guy.

"But where is it? I didn't wrap any paintings."

"The artist just finished it today. The paint's not even dry. I've got it hanging on a nail up in the attic."

"And what's Harry getting you? A ring?"

"No way!" she exclaimed. "He's been talking about it. And Lord knows, my grandparents are after me to let him make an honest woman of me, but after three trips to the altar, I still can't get used to the idea that marriage could be a good thing."

"It can be," I assured her. "And Harry's the one. The only. You can't judge marriage by what you had before. Those marriages don't even count."

"Bless you," BeBe said dryly. "Harry says the same thing. Only you have to consider the source."

I helped myself to a sip of BeBe's wine. "I'm just stumped when it comes to Daniel and Christmas," I said. "He doesn't need any new clothes. And usually he buys anything he needs before I even know it's something he'd like."

"Hmmm." She took the wineglass from me and sipped.

"Books?"

"He never has time to read anything except cookbooks, and he buys those himself."

"Music?"

"I did get him the new Eric Clapton CD. But that's the only thing I've bought for him."

"Cooking stuff?"

I shook my head. "He has enough gadgets to open a store of his own."

"Okay. I give up. You're right. He's impossible."

"It'll come to me," I said, though not really convinced. "But in the meantime, I'm having the best time playing Secret Santa."

"For who?" BeBe asked, getting up to turn down the flame on the gas logs in the fireplace.

"Apple Annie," I said, reaching into the shopping bag I'd brought along and dumping out its contents.

"That's not her real name," I explained. "I don't know her real name, so that's what I've been calling her."

"And how did you meet Miss Apple Annie?"

"I haven't. Not officially. But you have."

"Me?"

"At the open house at Maisie's Daisy," I said. "Remember the bag lady who was snitching cookies? Did I tell you, I think she came back and slept in the shop's display bed that night?"

"You never said a word!" BeBe said. "Is this the same woman who stole your blue Christmas tree pin? Are you insane?"

"I'm not insane," I said calmly. I reached into my pocketbook and held out my hand for her to inspect the contents.

"The pin! Where'd you get it?"

"She gave it back," I said. "Actually, I guess it was a swap. She took my daddy's BC letter sweater that night and in its place left her own sweater. With the Christmas tree brooch pinned to it."

"What's this about your playing Secret Santa to her?" BeBe said suspiciously.

"It's just little things," I said. "Nothing expensive. After that first morning, when I found the pin, I wanted to thank her for giving it back."

"Thank her for giving back what she'd stolen from you!" BeBe said. "Weezie, this woman broke into your house and stole food. Then she broke into the shop. Wait, how did she break in?"

"I don't know. It's the weirdest thing. The doors hadn't been jimmied. The locks hadn't been tampered with. And whenever she's come and gone, Jethro hasn't made a sound. That's why I'm pretty sure she's the same one who brought him back that night and locked him up in the truck. He trusts Annie."

"Annie!" BeBe hooted. "Has it occurred to you that this woman slept in your shop? Don't you think it's just possible that she's a crazy, lunatic stalker? She could let herself into your house at any time and slash you to ribbons, and Jethro would probably lick her foot and show her where the silver's hidden."

"Gee, BeBe," I said, my voice dripping sarcasm. "That thought hadn't occurred to me before, but I sure will sleep well now, thinking about that possibility."

"Weezie!" BeBe said, giving my shoulders a shake. "I'm serious. You shouldn't encourage this woman. You should call the cops and tell them what's going on."

"You sound just like Daniel," I said, calmly spreading out the contents of my shopping bag. "He's convinced she's some knife-wielding loony tune. He's such a cynic. Promise me you won't tell him about the Secret Santa thing."

"You are such an idiot," BeBe said.

"Promise," I begged.

"All right," she said grudgingly. "But don't come crying to me if you get murdered in your sleep."

She pointed at my heap of goodies. "What's all that?"

"Just some little treats for Annie," I said. "Hotel soaps and shampoos I've picked up on buying trips. A toothbrush and toothpaste. A pair of warm woolen socks. A candy bar. We know she has a sweet tooth! After I wrap them up, I put them in ziplock bags. So they won't get ruined in the rain."

"Of course," BeBe said in a mocking voice. "And where does Annie's Secret Santa leave her goodie bags?"

"You're making fun of me," I said.

"Absolutely," she agreed. "Best friend's prerogative. Where do you leave the stuff?"

"In the truck," I said. "Late at night. And it's always gone the next morning."

"Oh, there's a surprise," BeBe said. "You live in the historic district, which is headquarters for every homeless man in Savannah, and amazingly enough, when you leave stuff in your unlocked truck, it's gone the next day."

"I always put the presents in the glove box," I said. "Nobody but Annie would know to look there."

"Except for the army of homeless people who camp out in Colonial Cemetery, which is what? A block from your place? Anybody could be watching while you do your little Secret Santa thing."

"But they're not," I said stubbornly. "Annie is the only one who knows. Anyway, who else would leave presents for *me*?"

For once, BeBe was speechless. But only for a moment.

"A homeless woman leaves you gifts?"

"Wonderful gifts," I said. "Yesterday she left me a huge hotel key. From the old DeSoto Hotel."

"They tore that place down more than thirty-five years ago," BeBe said.

"I know. And she must know how I love anything from old Savannah," I said smugly.

"She probably stole it years ago," BeBe said flatly. "She was probably a hotel thief before she became a homeless thief. What else has she given you?"

"One morning, there was a huge pinecone. From a ponderosa pine, I think. It was the biggest pinecone I'd ever seen. Another time, it was the tiniest, most perfect little baby conch shell. No bigger than my thumbnail. But today's present was the best of all."

"I can't wait to hear," BeBe said in a perfect deadpan.

Ignoring her sarcasm, I reached back into my purse and brought out Apple Annie's gift.

"A bottle," BeBe said. "That's appropriate. For an old alkie."

"Not just any bottle," I said, turning the deep blue container over to show her the marking on the bottom. "This is a John Ryan soda bottle." With my fingertip I stroked the bottle, its finish worn to velvet.

"And?"

"Look at the date here," I instructed.

She scrunched up her eyes and examined the bottle's bottom.

"Eighteen sixty-seven. Is this thing really that old?"

"Yeah," I said softly. "You know I don't deal in old bottles. That's really more of a guy thing. But there are lots of bottle diggers and dealers around town. I know just enough about old bottles to know that I don't know enough. So I mostly leave them to the boys. Still . . ."

"This bottle is worth more than a million bucks," BeBe said. "And a homeless woman gave it to you. Just like that."

I gave her an annoyed look.

"I knew that John Ryan bottles were highly collectible," I said finally. "This one was filled with soda right here in Savannah. And yes, in 1867. So I did some research. It's *not* worth a million bucks. But the cobalt color is really desirable. This one, unfortunately, is missing the wire bail that would originally have been around the neck, to cap it. And there are some chips around the lip, and a hairline crack. I found a similar bottle on the Internet, that one was perfect. And it sold for ten thousand dollars."

"For an old soda bottle."

"I don't make the prices," I said. "I'm just telling you what the market is. Anyway, this bottle is nowhere near perfect. Not for a collector. But for me, I wouldn't take any money for it."

She sighed, picked up her wineglass, and drained it.

"You don't get it, I know," I said. "But Annie knows me. She knows I love anything that was made here in Savannah. Where *I* was made. And she knows blue is my favorite color. I think she must have found this somewhere. Maybe dug it up herself, somewhere around town, although that is totally illegal. But I don't care. It's the perfect Christmas gift."

"And it came from a wino," BeBe said.

"That's it!" I said, jumping up. I reached down, grabbed her hand, yanked her to a standing position, and gave her a huge hug.

"What?"

"Wine!" I said. "That's what I'll give Daniel. I got a flyer in the mail today. From Trader Bob. He never sends out flyers. But when he was up in the North Carolina mountains, he bought out this old guy's wine cellar. And he's selling all the wine bottles. Tomorrow morning! You know what a wine snob Daniel is. I'll run over there first thing tomorrow and buy him the best bottle of wine I can find."

"You don't know diddly about wine," BeBe said.

"No," I said, hugging her again. "But you do."

CHAPTER 14

I picked BeBe up at her place at eight the next morning. It had rained a little the night before, but this morning was sunny and colder than it had been earlier in the week. It really was beginning to feel like Christmas.

She walked unsteadily to the truck, and wobbled a little as she slid into the front seat, clutching a huge mug of coffee in one hand and a rolled-up magazine in the other.

"Not feeling well?" I asked, pulling away from the curb.

She shot me the look. "Do you know how much wine we put away last night?"

"A lot?"

"Three bottles. And I think I took care of more than my share."

"Sorry," I said.

"Not as sorry as me." She shuddered. "I don't think I can stand to look at another bottle of wine again. Ever."

"Well, you're going to," I said brightly. "Leuveda, she's Trader Bob's sister? There was a message from her on my answering machine when I got home last night. She says there are, like, two thousand bottles being auctioned off this morning."

BeBe closed her eyes and leaned her head back. "You are the only person in the world who could get me to go to a wine auction the way I'm feeling today."

I glanced over at the rolled-up magazine in her lap.

"Uh, BeBe? I don't think you're gonna have time to catch up on your reading at the auction. Trader Bob really moves these things along. And since I don't know a thing about wine—"

"Relax," she said, unrolling the magazine without opening her eyes. "This is *Wine Spectator*. Their annual price guide. It's research, sweetie."

"Oh. Good." I took a sip of my own coffee. "So. I've given it some thought, and here's what I've come up with. If the prices are decent, I'd like to buy two really good bottles of wine. A bottle of red—you know how much Daniel likes red wine—and a bottle of really good champagne."

"Champagne!" She moaned. "Oh, God. The only thing worse than a wine hangover is a champagne hangover."

"Forget hangover. Concentrate on helping me find Daniel a great Christmas present."

She opened one eye. "Red. Is that the best you can do? I mean, can you be a little more specific? Does he like bordeaux, burgundy, what?"

"Just red," I said. "You know me. I'll drink any old thing.

Daniel, on the other hand, likes the good stuff. So we're looking for something spectacular. Also the one thing I do know is the vintage."

"Yes?"

"Nineteen seventy," I said. "It's got to be a bottle from 1970."

"Impossible," she said flatly.

"Why?"

"There is no spectacular red wine from 1970," she said. "Pick another year, please."

"But I can't. That's the year he was born. It's the year I was born. It's got to be a 1970 vintage. Surely not everything from that year is awful?"

She yawned. "Well, it's certainly not 1961—the birth year of the most fabulously drinkable Château Latour—and the amazing Harry Sorrentino."

"What? Everything made that year sucks?"

She opened her eyes. "I didn't say they all suck. What I mean is, it wasn't a truly spectacular year, for the most part. Don't get your panties in a wad. I'm sure we'll find something drinkable at your little auction."

"Don't forget the champagne. I want a really nice bottle of champagne."

"Cristal's nice."

I made a face. "Isn't that what all the rappers and rock stars drink? I want something Daniel couldn't just pick up at Johnny Ganem's liquor store. Something for when we have something to celebrate."

"Hmm." Her eyes were closed again. "We'll see."

"I'm running out of time here," I reminded her. "Christmas is the day after tomorrow. And the whole family's coming over tomorrow night, and then I'm going to midnight mass."

Her eyes popped open again.

"Mass? Family?"

"I know," I said. "The mass thing is a Christmas gift for Mama. She's been saying novenas that I'll find my way back to the fold. So everybody, Jonathan and James and Miss Sudie, Mama and Daddy, is coming over to my house for supper on Christmas Eve. That's my gift to Daddy."

"Because?"

"That way he doesn't have to eat Mama's cooking for twenty-four hours. I've promised him a ham, and turkey, and oyster dressing and all the fixings. He'll have leftovers for days. And no heartburn, hopefully."

"Very Christian," BeBe said approvingly.

"And I want you and Harry to come over too," I said.

"Hmm."

"Please?" I tugged on the sleeve of her sweater. "At least for supper. That way, it won't be Daniel all alone with my bizarre family."

"Not everybody in your family is bizarre," she pointed out. "James is quite normal. And your daddy is a lovely man."

"But not a brilliant conversationalist. All Daddy ever talks to Daniel about is his old mailman war stories. And cars. You know Daniel doesn't give a rat's ass about cars. If you come, Daniel will have somebody else to talk to besides Daddy. And Mama—who keeps pumping him about when we're going to get married."

"Maybe," BeBe said. "I'll mention it to Harry. See what he thinks. I know we're definitely spending Christmas morning at my place. My grandparents are coming over, and I think one or more of my brothers may show up. And we're going out to the Breeze in the afternoon for an oyster roast, if the weather stays nice."

"Great," I said, beaming at her. "You'll even get a chance to meet Daniel's family."

"Daniel's family?" She raised an eyebrow.

"Derek and Eric and their wives and kids," I said. "It'll be the first time anybody in my family has met anybody from Daniel's."

"Does Daniel know about this?"

"It's a surprise," I said. "I've been planning it for weeks."

"All right," she said finally. "We'll come. I can't wait to see Daniel's family up close and personal after all these years."

"I'm getting a little nervous about it," I admitted. "It'll be a big help if you come."

"Great," she said, paging through her *Wine Spectator*. "I'll spend Christmas Eve refereeing the Foley Family Feud."

She spent the rest of the ride over to Hardeeville reading and dog-earing her magazine, and I spent the rest of the ride listening to Christmas carols on the oldies station I keep the truck radio tuned to.

"Ho-Lee Ca-rap," I said slowly as we pulled up to the parking lot at Trader Bob's.

A huge tractor-trailer rig was parked in the middle of the old cornfield, and at least fifty people were milling around the field. A makeshift wooden gangplank led from the field into the interior of the truck, and people were walking in and out of the trailer.

We parked, and I made my way through the crowd to a card table set up outside the door of the auction house. Leuveda Garner sat behind the table, wearing a fur Santa Claus hat and a moth-eaten mink stole. A stainless-steel coffee urn sat on the table beside her, along with a mountain of foam coffee cups. Folding chairs were stacked on the ground beside the table.

"Hey, Weezie!" she called out. "You got my message."

"I did," I agreed, looking around at the crowd. "Looks like a lot of other people did too. What's with the big rig?"

"That's the wine we're auctioning off," Leuveda said. "That whole truck is loaded to the rafters. There was so much of it, we didn't have time to unload everything. So Bob's just gonna set up and do his thing right there in front of the truck."

She handed both of us a thick sheaf of typed paper.

"This is the catalog," she said. "Don't pay any attention to my spelling. All those French words really had me flummoxed. You can walk up that ramp to the truck. We've got lights rigged in there, and you can take a look at the wine. Bob's got a helper in there, he can move the crates, if there's something in particular you want to see. "

BeBe was leafing through the catalog, running a finger down the listings. "Wow," she said admiringly. "There's some decent stuff here." She looked up at Leuveda. "Is any of it drinkable?"

Leuveda shrugged. "Don't know. Don't care. What you

see is what you get. We've never done a wine auction before. Bob only agreed to do this one as a favor to the family."

"Two thousand bottles of wine," I said, glancing down at my list. "And it all belonged to one guy?"

"Oh, this isn't even half of what he had in his basement and stashed around the house," Leuveda said. "We brought this much because it's all that would fit in the biggest truck we could rent. If this goes well, Bob may bring the other stuff down and auction it off after the holidays."

"Who has this much wine lying around his house?" BeBe asked, suspicious as always.

"A nut," Leuveda said promptly. "Wine nut, his family calls him. Of course, they had no idea he'd been collecting this much wine. He was kind of a shut-in. It wasn't until he got sick and had to be moved to a nursing home against his will that they discovered his whole house had been turned into a walk-in wine cellar. You should have seen the place, Weezie. He had the windows all covered with black cloth, and the thermostat set real low. Most of the furniture was gone. He had a bed and a recliner, and everything else was just cases and cases of wine."

"Sad," I said. But I had been to hundreds of estate sales over the years, and I had seen how a collecting mania could take over a person's life. Especially a person who was estranged from any kind of outside life or interests.

"Yeah," Leuveda agreed. "Funny thing is, the poor guy didn't even drink. He came from a family of real foot-washing fundamentalists. The wine was his idea of an investment plan. Of course, now he's dead, and the foot-washing fundamentalists are mortified about having to get rid of all that sinful wine."

BeBe laughed. "I'll bet they'll be willing to spend the money y'all make selling the wine though."

"Of course," Leuveda agreed. "Money talks, bullshit walks."

From the other side of the field, we heard a buzz of static electricity, then the voice of Trader Bob Gross booming through the mists still rising from the field.

"All right, folks," he called. "What was it those Gallo brothers said? We will sell no wine before its time? Well, it's high time, folks. So let's sell some wine."

"I'll get our chairs and set them up front as close as I can get," I told BeBe. "Why don't you run over to the trailer and take a look to see if any of it looks any good?"

"Okay," she said, seeming dubious. "I can look, but if they won't let us take a taste, all I'll be going on is the appearance of the bottles and the corks."

While BeBe sprinted toward the tractor trailer, I took two chairs and set them up in what was becoming the second row for the auction. I exchanged greetings and nods with other auction regulars I knew—Janet, the Hummel lady, who always showed up to bid on Hummel porcelain figurines with a stack of price guides in tow; Waldo, a long-haired hippie type who usually bid on comic books, old records, or any kind of toy or board game related to sixties or seventies television shows; and, inevitably, Kitty, the knitting lady. I didn't know any of these people's full names of course, and I'd made up Kitty's name, but this was as far as our auction relationship went.

I tried reading the wine listings, but none of it meant anything to me, with the exception of a Château Margaux listing, which I recognized because I'd read somewhere that Margaux Hemingway had been named for the wine her parents drank the night she was conceived.

Just as Bob was tapping his microphone for the second time to signal that he was about to start the auction, BeBe came strolling up.

"We're good," she said tersely, looking around to see if anybody was eavesdropping.

"You found a wine for me to bid on?"

"Mmm-hmm. Absolutely," she said. "Now, pay attention. If they auction the wine in the order it's listed—"

"He will. Bob always does things in order."

"Okay. Well, this bottle is listed number twelve. So pay attention. Get that bid paddle of yours ready to rock and roll."

"That good, huh?"

"It's a 1970 Château Pétrus pomerol," BeBe whispered. "*Wine Spectator* rates it a must buy."

"Right year, right color," I said, nodding approval.

"There's just one thing I should tell you," she added. "It's not cheap."

"This is Daniel's Christmas present," I said. "Money is no object."

"Good," she said. "Because the last bottle anybody bought of this particular vintage, they paid a thousand bucks for it."

CHAPTER 15

Folks," Trader Bob intoned, "here's the ground rules for today's auction. All bottles of wine are sold 'as is' with no guarantees on my part that any of it will taste any damn good."

Chuckles and guffaws rippled through the field. The sun was out, but it was chilly, and I was glad of my heavy denim barn jacket with the big patch pockets, where I'd stashed a couple of granola bars and my checkbook and billfold.

"Due to the nature of this auction, and by request of the estate's family," he continued, "we're operating on a strictly cash-and-carry basis. What that means is, what you buy today, you take away today. And we will not be accepting checks or credit cards."

"No!" I gasped. BeBe glanced over in alarm.

"They always take checks," I said. "And the flyer didn't say anything about cash only. Well . . . shit."

"Also," Bob said, "nothing except coffee and sodas are to be consumed on our premises today because I don't want the sheriff on my tail."

He reached out to one of the helpers who were busily surrounding him with a growing hill of cardboard wine cartons and took a slender green bottle that he held up to the light.

"Let's start with this little beauty right here. It's a . . ." He frowned, pushed his glasses to the end of his nose, and squinted at the label.

"Ah, hell," he said finally. "It's bottle number one, lot one, listed right there on your catalog."

BeBe rolled her eyes and grimaced. "Liebfraumilch. And a strictly mediocre one, at that. It's a good thing the guy who bought this stuff died before he had to start living off his wine investments."

"We got three cases of this stuff here," Bob said smoothly. "And I'll take one money for all three. Let's see. That's twelve bottles a case, thirty-six bottles, let's say thirty bucks a bottle."

"Let's don't," BeBe said.

"Round it to a thousand bucks for the lot," Bob said. "Come on. One money, thirty-six bottles of pure drinking pleasure. Who'll give me a K?"

The field was quiet.

"Twenty a bottle?" Bob asked. "Seven eighty. Gimme seven eighty."

Trader Bob cupped his hand to his ear. "Mighy quiet out there. Are y'all awake, or sleepin' one off?"

He exchanged a questioning look with Leuveda.

"Don't ask me," she drawled. "You know I drink Cold Duck, my ownself."

"Gimme ten," Bob urged. "Ya can't hardly buy nothin' for that these days. And think of all the Christmas joy you could be spreading."

The crowd's reaction was a deafening indifference. In fact, the only thing I heard, aside from BeBe's snort of derision, was the steady, hypnotic clicking of Kitty the knitter's needles.

"Five?" Bob clutched his hand to his chest, as though a knife were being thrust through it, but still no bid paddles were extended.

"All right," he said finally, a beaten man. "We got a lot of wine to move this morning. Let's get this thing rolling. Somebody gimme an offer."

"Five bucks a case, Bob," called a gnomish man standing off to the right. He wore a set of green camouflage coveralls and a bright orange Elmer Fudd cap with fur earflaps.

"Fifteen bucks for all that delicious fruit of the vine?"

Elmer Fudd nodded and held up his paddle to officially register the bid.

"All right. We got fifteen. Gimme sixteen," Bob chanted. Paddles went up. Bob's chant accelerated until he'd gaveled the first lot down for an underwhelming thirty-six dollars, or as Bob put it, "a pitiful buck a bottle."

BeBe nodded her approval.

The next few lots of wine didn't fare much better. The top individual bottle sold for sixty bucks, and to get that, Trader

Bob, wheedled, cajoled, and once threatened to walk off his podium, "And call the whole damned thing off."

Through it all, BeBe alternated glances between her well-thumbed copy of *Wine Spectator* and the catalog, noting each winning bid in the catalog with her slender silver Mont Blanc pen.

"This is looking good," she said after the tenth lot had sold. "That last case of chenin blanc should have brought at least thirty bucks a bottle."

"But the whole case only went for two hundred dollars," I pointed out. "So I should get my bottle cheap, right?"

"Hopefully. Of course, that chenin blanc is sort of a sleeper. Not a lot of people have heard of the winery it came from. Unfortunately, the wine we want is quite well known and sought after. It's one of the classiest ones they're selling off today. So it could be that everybody's just holding out, waiting for the good stuff to come up."

I turned around in my chair to appraise the competition, and was surprised to see that the crowd had grown appreciably since the auction started. All seventy or so chairs were full, and more people were milling around the trailer and standing at the back of the rows of chairs.

My heart sank when I saw a familiar Burberry plaid tam-o'-shanter.

"Shit," I exclaimed, slapping my thigh with the rolled-up catalog.

"What?" BeBe turned and craned her neck.

"Cookie Parker is here," I said. "And Manny. I should have guessed they'd somehow find out about this."

"Which ones are they?" she asked, half standing to get a better scan of the crowd.

"Standing right by the trailer," I said. "Cookie's wearing a goofy plaid hat and a tan coat with a fur collar. And Manny's the one in the—"

"—tightest blue jeans I have ever seen on a grown man," BeBe exclaimed, openly staring. "Also the gaudiest cowboy shirt ever made. Sequins before noon! Who *are* these guys?"

"My worst nightmare," I said gloomily. "Gay guys with money."

"And questionable taste," she added, standing up. "We'll just see about this."

"Wait," I said. "What are you going to do? My wine is coming up pretty soon."

"You just concentrate on buying that pomerol," BeBe instructed. "According to the catalog, there are three bottles of it and they'll each be sold separately."

"How high should I bid?" I asked, suddenly unnerved by the prospect of bidding in such unfamiliar territory.

"How much cash did you bring?"

I dug in my jacket pocket and brought out a wad of bills, which I quickly counted.

"Looks like one hundred seventeen dollars," I wailed. "Not enough. Not nearly enough."

"I've got two hundred right here," she said, patting her pocketbook. "Think of me as your own personal ATM."

"But you said the last bottle sold for a thousand bucks."

"At a black-tie charity auction in Sonoma Valley, California," she said. "Whereas, *we* are standing in a cornfield in

Hardeeville, South Carolina. Don't spend more than three hundred dollars. There's still a bottle of champagne, a Krug blanc de blanc Clos de Mesnil, 1985, that I've got my eye on. It's on the third page, and it won't be cheap."

"It doesn't matter," I said, slumping down in my metal chair. "Manny and Cookie will be bidding up everything. We might as well leave right now."

"Is there any coffee left in your thermos?" she asked.

"Yeah, it's still half full," I said, wondering what this had to do with my current predicament. I unscrewed the cap and sniffed the steam rising from the vacuum jug.

"Gimme," she said.

I handed over the thermos. "Leave it up to me," BeBe said, giving me a wink. "I always get my man."

She shrugged out of her own flannel-lined jean jacket and I shivered on her behalf. The wind had picked up a little, and the sun was suddenly playing hide-and-go-seek behind a bank of clouds. The sky was cold, and promising, if not snow, some nasty icy rain.

I watched while she sashayed across the field in the direction of the trailer and the Babalu boys. She saw me watching and jerked her head in the direction of Trader Bob, reminding me that I needed to pay attention to the ongoing auction.

Bob finished hammering down a half case of a wine I'd never heard of and was pausing to read off the description of the lot I'd been waiting for.

"Folks," he drawled, "this next wine is the real deal."

Heads jerked to attention. My own hand clenched the bid paddle so tightly I felt my fingertips go numb.

"This here," he said, holding up a bottle to the light, "is the kind of wine they tell me is one of a kind. It's a bordeaux. That much I can pronounce. And it's got a pedigree out the ying-yang. They say a bottle of this stuff here will sell for a thousand bucks."

"Yeah. In your dreams, Gross," yelled one of the hecklers standing by the trailer, his fists jammed into the front pockets of his jeans.

Bob shrugged. "All right. I figger somebody out there is an educated wine connoisseur. And that somebody will be willing to pay the price for a one-of-a-kind bottle of bordeaux. We got three bottles, and I'm selling 'em for one money. Y'all can keep one, sell the others off, whatever you want. But I'm looking for twenty-five hundred dollars. That's way less than the going price."

His head swiveled to and fro, surveying the bidders. I turned and tried not to stare at Cookie and Manny, who had their heads together, in rapt discussion about something. BeBe stood off to the side, watching them intently.

"Two thousand?" Bob asked.

The crowd was quiet, but I heard a distinct, low-level buzz. People were interested, trying to decide when the time was right to jump in.

"I'll give you fifty, Bob," Kitty hollered, holding up her paddle in one hand, but not bothering to drop her knitting.

"Fifty?" Bob sounded wounded. "For that, I'll take it home and drink it myself."

"Ya gotta start somewhere," Leuveda advised. "Or we'll be here all day."

"Sixty," somebody in the back yelled.

"Seventy-five," called Waldo the hippie.

The bids were coming fast and furious now, and Bob was straining to keep up.

It stalled out a little when the bidding hit $150, and for the first time I raised my paddle.

"Weezie, got you at one fifty," Bob called, nodding his approval.

"One sixty." I recognized Cookie's voice instantly.

Gritting my teeth, I nodded at Bob. "One seventy."

"One eighty." This time it was Manny doing the bidding. Bob cocked an eyebrow at me.

I nodded. "One ninety."

A woman's voice called out from the front. "Two hundred."

Damn, now it wasn't just the Babalu boys bidding me up.

"Two ten," Cookie called.

"Two twenty," the woman said coolly.

I bit my lip. "Two thirty."

I glanced over at Manny and Cookie just in time to see BeBe sashay past in the most casual of manners. Suddenly though, she tripped on something, and I saw, as though in slow motion, the coffee thermos go flying up in the air. Now a stream of hot coffee was raining down on Cookie.

A shrill, high-pitched scream pierced the air. Heads turned.

"Two forty?" Bob asked, impervious to pain or injury or anything else that distracted from a sale. "Anybody for two forty?"

I was too stunned to do anything but watch. BeBe had picked herself up off the ground and was now busily trying to blot coffee off Cookie's chest.

"Leave me *alone!*" Cookie cried. "Ohmygod. This coat is cashmere."

"It's ruined!" Manny chimed in.

"Two forty," the woman in the front row called.

I glanced over at BeBe, who jerked her head in the direction of Bob.

"Two fifty," I prompted.

"I'm so sorry," I heard BeBe wail. She stuck a pencil and a pad in Cookie's face. "Here. Write down your phone number. I'll pay for the cleaning. I'll replace the coat."

"He's burned!" Manny wailed, pulling Cookie's damp shirt away from his chest. "I think we need a doctor."

"Two sixty," my new female nemesis called, sounding bored with the whole drama.

Bob cocked his head. "Weezie?"

"Two seventy," I said, reminding myself that this was Daniel's Christmas present. Out of the corner of my eye, I saw Manny hustle Cookie off in the direction of the parking lot.

"Three hundred!" the woman in front called triumphantly.

I closed my eyes for a moment and gave it some deep thought. If I went any higher, there was no guarantee I'd win the bordeaux. And there was still the champagne to consider. Maybe by the time it came up, the crowd would have thinned out, and I'd get it at a bargain. Maybe.

"Weezie?" Bob asked.

I kept my eyes closed and shook my head no.

"Three hundred fifty!"

It was BeBe's voice. I opened my eyes and saw her striding up the aisle in my direction. Her shirt was soaked with coffee, and she had that look in her eye.

"Three sixty?" Bob asked.

Silence.

"All right then," Bob said quickly. "Three fifty once, twice, sold! To—"

BeBe grabbed my bid paddle and held it triumphantly over her head.

CHAPTER 16

The first drops of rain started falling as I counted out our hard-won cash to Leuveda, including two crumpled twenty-dollar bills that BeBe pulled from a secret compartment in her right boot.

"Don't ask," she said darkly, when I was about to. "Ever since my episode with poverty, I go nowhere without a couple twenties tucked in my shoe for a rainy day."

I glanced up at the charcoal-tinged sky and flipped up the hood on my jacket. "And this definitely looks like it's going to be one of those days."

"Here," I said, shoving one of the bottles at BeBe, along with the keys to the truck. "Get the heater going. I'll be back in a few minutes."

A few turned into twenty, and it had started to drizzle, but when I climbed into the driver's seat, it was with a smug grin on my face and the bottle of champagne tucked inside my jacket.

"What took so long?" she grumped.

I handed her the Krug and two twenties and started to thread my way out of the lot.

"How?"

"I sold off the other two bottles of bordeaux to the woman who was bidding against me," I said. "For two hundred bucks. I had to go eighty to get the Krug."

She shook her head in admiration. "And you still broke even. Weezie Foley, you are a mess!"

By the time we were on the road, the rain was coming down hard and the temperature had dropped at least twenty degrees.

BeBe shivered and buttoned her jean jacket up over her bra. "What I wouldn't give for some of that hot coffee right now," she said through chattering teeth.

"Was Cookie really burned?" I asked, wincing at the memory of his screams.

"No way," she assured me. "I left the top off the thermos for five minutes. It was barely lukewarm. He's just a big ol' baby. Gay or not, did you ever meet a man who wasn't a big ol' baby?"

"You're the authority," I agreed.

BeBe turned up the heat a notch and sat back and rubbed her hands in glee. "Anyway, we both did what we had to do. I can't believe you got the wine *and* the champagne. It's a fabulous gift. Daniel will love it."

"He'd better," I said. "Anyway, that's a huge load off my mind. Now I'm done. My last Christmas gift!."

"Speaking of gifts," she said. "What did you get from Annie?"

"Annie?" My mind was a blank.

"Apple Annie. Your charity case."

"Jeez," I said. "With the excitement of the auction, I completely forgot to look. Open the glove box and see what's in there."

I glanced over once, but mostly kept my eyes on the road. Driving over the humpbacked Talmadge Memorial Bridge that crosses the Savannah River gives me a bad case of the heebie-jeebies on a good day, but now with the rain and the gusting winds, I was more nervous than usual.

BeBe punched the lock on the glove box and brought out a festive red plaid gift bag tied with a jaunty black velvet bow.

"Hey," she said, holding it in front of me. "Look. Apple Annie's got your gift-wrapping gene."

I frowned. "That's not *for* me. It's *from* me. Look again. Is there anything else in there?"

BeBe rummaged around in the glove box and held up her findings. "Screwdriver."

"Check."

"Flashlight."

"Check."

"Hoo-hoo!" she chortled, bringing out a small cardboard box. "Condoms! Annie must know you better than I thought."

"Give me those," I said, snatching the box away from her and stashing it under my seat.

"I take it those are also not from Annie?" BeBe asked in a teasing singsong.

"Not another word."

"Well, there's nothing else in the glove box," she concluded, shutting it.

"I don't understand," I said. "The truck was unlocked. Why didn't she take her gift?"

"Maybe she was busy getting her hair and nails done for the Symphony fund-raiser," BeBe quipped.

I shot her a dirty look, but BeBe just tossed her hair and fidgeted with the top button on her jean jacket.

"This isn't like Annie," I went on. "I've been leaving her those little presents every night for a week. And she hasn't missed picking them up. Not once. Till now."

"You're worried," BeBe said, rolling her eyes, "about a bag lady."

I nodded agreement, my mind already filling with a variety of possibilities to explain the gift's presence in my truck. None of them were pleasant.

"You think something bad could have happened to her," BeBe went on.

"She lives on the streets!" I exclaimed. "Of course I'm worried. She could be hurt. Or sick . . ."

"Or drunk. Look, Weezie, you said it yourself. This is Apple Annie we're talking about here. She's a street person. Maybe she just hit the road. Anyway, you don't know anything about her. Not really. So don't go making yourself sick worrying and inventing all kinds of tragic scenarios about why she didn't pick up her little care package."

I chewed at the inside of my mouth and stared out the windshield as the wipers sliced through ribbons of rain. I drummed my fingertips on the steering wheel.

BeBe sighed and shifted in her seat.

"You're not going to just forget about her, are you? You're going to make some desperate, well-intentioned, but totally futile attempt to track her down and patch her up. Aren't you?"

I stared straight ahead.

"She's not a stray kitten," BeBe warned. "Weezie, these street people live that way because they want to, most of 'em. They're fiercely independent and they totally resent any efforts to change their lifestyle."

I rolled my eyes.

"She's a human being," BeBe went on. "A complex and probably deeply screwed-up human being. You can't fix her."

"But it's Christmas," I blurted out. "Look, I know she's not some house cat I can just feed a bowl of milk to and tie a ribbon around her collar. I *know* that. But I can't help it. Yes, I'm worried about Annie. It's not like her to completely miss picking up her present. Or to miss leaving one for me. I swear, I don't want to fix her or adopt her. I just want to give her a lousy bag of soap and shampoo and some candy. Is that so awful?"

"Not if you're able to just leave it at that," BeBe said. "Anyway, if you want to give her something she can really use, you should have bought some of that rotgut buck-a-bottle wine back there in Hardeeville."

"Screw you, Ebenezer." I said it softly, mostly under my breath, but definitely loud enough to be heard.

We were just turning onto Charlton Street when BeBe finally spoke again.

"All right," she said with a martyred sigh. "I give up. Where do we start looking for Apple Annie?"

"The women's shelter," I said promptly. "You check there. I'll drive over to Reynolds Square, and then over to Franklin Square, where those homeless guys always hang out. If you find her, don't talk to her. Just call me on my cell phone."

She gave me a mock salute. "Aye-aye, captain."

CHAPTER 17

I drove slowly around Reynolds Square, looking for Apple Annie. But the square was deserted. Not even a pigeon would have braved this cold and rain.

The thought occurred to me, as I headed north to Franklin Square—where *do* homeless people go in this kind of weather? It was too early for the shelters to open yet. And for that matter, where do pigeons go when the weather's gruesome?

Franklin Square, which stood at the edge of Savannah's revitalized City Market district, wasn't any livelier than Reynolds Square. The homeless men who usually congregated on the park benches, playing checkers on upended buckets, had disappeared.

I sighed and headed slowly around the square. I spent the next hour cruising every downtown street and lane, looking for Annie.

Finally, when I was passing the soup kitchen at Emmaus House, on Abercorn Street, I noticed two shabbily dressed men crouching under the building's overhang, trying to stay dry.

I parked the truck illegally in front of a fire hydrant, and splashed through the puddles toward them.

The men were both white, but their faces were so caked with grime and their shabby knitted caps pulled so low over their foreheads, it was impossible to guess their ages.

"Excuse me," I said breathlessly. "I'm looking for a friend of mine. She's an older lady who, uh, lives on the streets around here."

"Yeah?" The shorter of the two men, whose cap was faded red, took his sock-covered hands out of his pockets and rubbed them together. "What's she done?"

"Nothing!" I said. "I've, uh, got something I need to give her. But she's not around. I wonder if either of you have seen her? Maybe here at the soup kitchen?"

The taller man, whose hat was olive drab, coughed roughly, and I jumped backward, instinctively.

He wiped his nose with his bare hand. "What's this lady look like?"

That gave me pause. I'd actually only glimpsed Annie once, that night of the open house at Maisie's Daisy.

"She's a white lady," I said hesitantly. "Probably in her sixties. Gray hair . . ."

"And?" Green Hat said impatiently, pulling a mangled half-smoked cigarette out of his pocket and lighting it with an orange plastic lighter.

Suddenly I remembered another, telling detail.

"She might be wearing a maroon BC letter sweater."

Green Hat exhaled smoke in my face, then coughed again.

Cringing, I took another step backward.

"I'd remember better—" he said thoughtfully.

"—if we had some money," his red-hatted friend said, finishing the idea.

"Oh." I fished in my jacket pocket, then remembered, belatedly, Daniel's advice about giving handouts to homeless men.

I brought out the granola bars I'd stashed in my pocket for breakfast.

"I'm kinda broke," I said, flashing an apologetic grin. "But you can have these. They're chocolate chip and peanut butter. Protein, you know?"

"No, thanks," Red Hat snarled. "We're trying to cut back on sweets."

"Yeah," the smoker said. "We gotta watch our girlish figures."

I shrugged and started to turn away. "Sorry."

"Too bad," Red Hat said. He knocked on his forehead. "Aw, look. I forgot where I saw your lady friend. Earlier. Like maybe half an hour ago."

"You saw her?" I turned back. "Where?"

"We forget," the smoker said. He took a last drag on his cigarette and tossed the butt at my feet. It hit a puddle and sizzled a moment before dying out.

"That's not very nice," I said, giving them a reproachful look. "It's Christmas, you know."

"Yeah," Red Hat said. "We know."

"Well—" I sputtered, trying to think of a clever come-back. "Merry Christmas!"

The smoker stepped forward menacingly, and I turned and ran for the safety of the truck, locking the doors as soon as I slid onto the seat.

I was almost home before I noticed the white rectangle of paper stuck in the corner of my windshield.

"Damn," I cried. "Another stinking parking ticket."

It was past one by the time I pushed open the front door at Maisie's Daisy.

Mary, the blond-haired UGA student who sometimes helped out around the shop when she was home from school, looked up from the magazine she was reading. "Hey, Weezie," she called. "Wow. You're soaked."

"Pretty much," I agreed. I shrugged out of my jacket and pulled off my equally sodden boots and headed for the back room to try to dry off.

"Anything going on around here?" I called to her.

"Not much. It's been raining so hard, not a single person came in all morning."

I emerged from the back room with a towel wrapped around my wet hair.

"Figures," I said. "You can go on home if you want, Mary. I think I'll close up early. Nobody with any sense is coming out in this mess."

"Okay." She hopped down from the wooden stool behind the counter, grabbed her purse, and headed for the door.

"Wait." I opened the cash register drawer and took out a twenty, which I tried to hand her.

"Oh no," she protested. "You don't need to pay me. I

didn't do anything except read your magazines. The phone didn't even ring."

"I insist," I said, pressing the bill into her hands. "So nobody came by at all? You didn't happen to see a little homeless lady hanging around outside? Maybe wearing an old BC letter sweater?"

Her big blue eyes widened. "An old lady in a letter sweater? No, I didn't see anybody like that."

After Mary left, I wandered around the shop, doing some light dusting, straightening shelves, and making a list of merchandise I'd put on my After Christmas Clearance table.

The blue lights twinkled on the aluminum tree, and my retro Christmas tunes played away on the shop's CD player, but I somehow couldn't shake the melancholy that settled over me like a mist.

I kept a close watch on the sidewalk in front of the shop, and a couple times even went to the back door to look out to the lane, which was just as quiet. It was futile, I knew, but I still hoped maybe Annie would reappear.

It was nearly four when my cell phone rang. I ran to answer it.

"No go on the women's shelter," BeBe reported. "And they've never even seen a woman who fits the description I gave them of Annie. They said most of their 'guests' are younger."

"Okay," I said with a sigh. "I didn't find her either. I did find two guys in front of the soup kitchen at Emmaus House who tried to extort money from me in exchange for information. But they probably didn't really know her."

"Probably not," BeBe agreed. She hesitated. "You're not

going to let this Apple Annie thing turn into a full-blown obsession, are you?"

"No. You're probably right. I'm just going to forget about her."

"I'm definitely right," BeBe said. "Now go home and wrap some Christmas presents."

"I've only got two left to wrap," I reminded her. "But I am going to close up early and start cooking for tomorrow night."

"Thatta girl," she said. "What time do you want us?"

"Dinner's at eight. But you could come early and help keep Mama out of the kitchen."

"Just as long as you don't make me eat any of that fruit-cake," she promised.

I was standing at the front door, with my keys in hand, ready to lock up, when a tall woman in a rusty black ankle-length raincoat came dashing up out of nowhere.

"Don't tell me you're closed!" she wailed, spying the keys.

"Sorry." I flashed her a regretful smile.

"Please?" She pushed a damp strand of graying red hair out of her eyes. "I left work early just to come over here. I walk by every night on my way home, but you're always closed by then."

She pointed toward the display window. "The record player. How much is it?"

"Sorry," I repeated. "It's actually just a display piece. It's not for sale."

"Oh no." Her shoulders drooped.

"You can get very nice repro turntables at Restoration

Hardware now," I said helpfully. "Or you could probably buy one on eBay."

"No time," she said sorrowfully. "My bus leaves for Buffalo in a couple hours. I wanted it for my older sister," she explained. "She's got all these records, from when she was a teenager. They're the old forty-fives, but she's got nothing to play them on. Dad gave away her record player years ago, after my mom died and he sold the house."

"Oh." I didn't know what else to say.

"It's okay," she said. "I've got some perfume for her, and a book. She likes mysteries. Nothing gory. She likes romance novels better, but her husband left this summer. Took off with his twenty-eight-year-old secretary. So I don't want anything too sappy. Of course, everything makes her cry these days."

"What kind of music does your sister like?" I asked, unlocking the door and holding it open.

"Huh?"

"Come on," I said, shooing her inside. "If you're going to take the turntable, you might as well take the records too. How about Elvis? Does she like Elvis?"

The woman stood in the doorway of the shop, rain streaming onto the floor.

"Are you kidding? She loves Elvis. Chuck Berry. The Platters. Tams, Temptations."

I scooped the record player off the display bed in the window and took it and the records over to the cash register. I found a gift box under the counter, popped the record player inside it, and placed the records on top.

"Pick out your gift paper," I instructed, pointing to the rack of papers behind me. "Pink poodles? Penguins? Christmas trees?"

"Linda would love the red plaid," the woman said promptly. "She's still got her old red plaid lunchbox from when we were kids."

"To Linda," I wrote the name on the card with a flourish. "From?"

"Nancy," she said, reaching for her purse. "My name's Nancy. This is so sweet of you. Really. I can't thank you enough. How much?"

"It's on me," I said, feeling the melancholy melt away as quickly as it had come. I tied on a huge green velvet bow. "Merry Christmas."

CHAPTER 18

Daniel let himself in the back door of my town house around midnight, right as I was taking the last two pies—a pecan and an apple—out of the oven.

"Hey," I said, pleased and surprised to see him this early. Christmas business at the restaurant had been so hectic, he sometimes didn't get in until two or three in the morning.

"Hey, yourself," he said, touching a practiced fingertip to the crust of the already cooling lemon pound cake on a cake stand. He nodded approval.

Daniel kissed me briefly, then sat down at the counter, surveying my kitchen. All evening, I'd checked numerous times to see if Annie had shown up to collect her gift, my anxiety feeding a burst of nervous energy that I'd poured into chopping, stirring, and sautéing.

The counters were covered with cakes, pies, and casseroles, not to mention a big pan of oyster dressing and a giant bowl of navel oranges which I'd spent the last hour peeling and cutting up for ambrosia.

"What's all this?" he asked, pouring himself a glass of red wine.

"Christmas dinner," I said, holding out my own glass for a refill.

"Did you invite the whole street? I mean, there's enough food here for Pharaoh's army."

"You know how I always overcook," I said lightly. "Mama says it's a sin to let a guest leave your table hungry."

"Eloise?" Daniel put down his wineglass. There were two bright spots of red on his cheeks. "Just how many people did you invite over for dinner?"

"Not that many," I said, busily grating coconut into the cut-glass bowl for the ambrosia. "Just family and a couple friends."

"Whose family? The Osmonds? This is a serious shitload of food here. And I seem to remember that you're an only child."

"Yes, but besides you and me and Mama and Daddy, there'll be Uncle James and Jonathan, of course, and Miss Sudie. And BeBe and Harry are coming, and Derek and Eric—"

"Whoa," he said sternly. "You invited my brothers for Christmas dinner without consulting me?"

"And their wives and kids," I said quickly, getting it out of the way.

"That's not a family dinner," he said. "It's a traveling freak show."

"It's Christmas. I just thought it would be nice to have both our families for dinner. Is that a crime? Our families have never met."

"Why do they have to meet? Ever?"

Quietly I set the coconut down on a clean plate. I wiped my hands on a dish towel. I took a deep breath.

"Our families need to meet each other because you and I are in a serious, committed relationship. Aren't we?"

"So far."

I ignored that.

"This will be my first Christmas cooking dinner in my own house. Every other year my mother has cooked. And before that, in the bad old days, when I was married to Tal, his mother cooked Christmas dinner." I shuddered involuntarily at the memory of those silent, chilly dinners in the Evans family dining room.

"Finger bowls," I said suddenly.

"Huh?"

"Tal's mother used to set the table as though the duke and duchess of Windsor were expected. Right down to finger bowls. Crystal knife rests, place cards. Four different forks, two knives, and three wineglasses. It was grotesque. I could never eat a bite without worrying she'd catch me using the wrong fork, or dropping peas on her Aubusson carpet."

I took another deep breath. "This year, I wanted to do something special. I know how you feel about Christmas. I know it has all kinds of bitter associations for you. And I want to change that. I want to make a beautiful holiday dinner for the person I love most in the world. For you. You're my family. And your family is my family."

I felt a little weak-kneed after finally giving my big speech, the one I'd been practicing in my head for days now.

"All right," he said finally. "If this means so much to you, I guess I can go along with it."

I leaned over and kissed his cheek.

"It won't be so bad. I promise. It'll be fun!"

"Like a root canal."

"Daniel!"

"Look. Eric's kids won't eat anything except dinner rolls, white rice, and vanilla ice cream," he said. "Their mother, Ellen, caters to this absurd behavior. And Derek's wife, Sondra, is diabetic. Not to mention a practicing vegan."

I smiled serenely. "I know all about your family's dietary peculiarities. Sondra faxed over a list of foods that are acceptable to her. I just left the butter and cream out of a couple dishes, and I fixed some pumpkin bars that are made with applesauce, instead of eggs. Also Eric volunteered to bring his kids' favorite rice dish, as well as the ice cream. See? I have everything under control."

"You wish," he said. "Did Sondra happen to mention that she and Ellen haven't spoken to each other since *last* Christmas, when Ellen had too much eggnog and told Sondra she needed to gain some weight because she was starting to look like an anorexic crack whore?"

I swallowed hard. "Uh, no. That didn't come up."

He gave me an evil grin. "It will. You might want to think

about writing up some place cards of your own, to keep those two from having a catfight."

He poured himself another glass of wine, topped off my glass, then stood up and took me by the hand.

"Come on, Eloise Foley. It's getting late. Let's go sit by the fire in front of that Christmas tree of yours and see if you can't put me in the holiday mood."

"Be right there," I promised. "Save me a seat. I just need to run out to the truck and check on something."

"In the truck?" He frowned. "At this time of night?"

"I had my arms full of groceries when I came in," I fibbed. "And I left the last bag in the front seat."

"I'll get it," he said, turning toward the kitchen door.

"No!" I said quickly. "It's, uh, a Christmas gift for you. A surprise."

"All right, but don't forget to lock the truck before you come in. I'm still not comfortable with all the weird things that have been going on around here lately."

I grabbed a sweater from a hook by the back door and hurried out to the truck. Opening the passenger-side door, I popped the lock on the glove box, still hoping.

But the red plaid bag, with its jaunty bow, was untouched.

I left the bag where it was and closed the door. I stood by the truck, wrapping my arms around myself for warmth. "Annie," I called softly. "Come out, come out, wherever you are."

CHAPTER 19

I smoothed my grandmother's starched white damask cloth over the battered pine harvest table in the dining room, and with my fingertips, traced the tiny patches where she'd so painstakingly mended it. If I looked closely, and I did, I could see the faintest ghost outlines of stains from family dinners long ago.

The pale pink splotch on one corner, I was sure, was the remnant of a red wine spill, probably from one of the bad uncles at Thanksgiving dinner. There were numerous small grease stains—my Meemaw served gravy on everything— even eggs. There was a single scorch mark near the middle of the rectangular cloth, and this, Mama had told me, was the result of my sixth birthday party, when I'd blown out the candles on my cake with such gusto that I'd sent one candle flying onto the tablecloth, where Daddy had extinguished the resulting flame with the remnants from a coffee cup.

I had plenty of beautiful linens I could have set the table with that night. Years of dealing and collecting old textiles had yielded a closet full of them. I'd considered using the gorgeous Irish linen cloth with the hand-tatted convent lace that had been a wedding gift to Mama, who, saving it for "nice," had never once used it before handing it down to me at my own ill-fated wedding to Talmadge Evans III.

But Meemaw's tablecloth, with all those tangible re-minders of happy family occasions, was the only one that would do for such a special night.

Circling the table, I dealt out the dishes, not fine bone china, which I had plenty of as well, but instead, my favorite flow blue china in a pattern called Claremont, by Johnson Brothers.

I'd found three of the flow blue dinner plates years and years ago at the Junior League Thrift Shop in Atlanta, when Tal was still in school at Georgia Tech. At two dollars apiece, they were a big splurge at the time. Over the years, I'd man-aged to fill out those original plates to a service for twelve. I rarely buy Claremont anymore, though, as the plates now sell for close to $150 apiece.

We'd actually have thirteen at the grown-up table tonight, but I had another flow blue plate, from a different but similar pattern, that I would put at my own place at the table.

After the china was placed, I added etched wineglasses from several different patterns, and topped each plate with a heavy damask banquet-size napkin with a gorgeous rococo monogrammed *W*, and added my wedding silver, which I'd stubbornly kept buying long after my wedding was history.

I placed two cut-glass bowls of white roses down the center of the table and scattered about my collection of sterling candlesticks, no two of which matched.

"Wow," BeBe said, popping her head in from the kitchen. "It's beautiful, Weezie. Like a painting or something."

"It's not too fancy?" I asked anxiously, remembering those dreaded stiff dinners in the Evans family dining room.

"Elegant, but not off-putting," she declared, dragging in two of the wooden folding chairs she was loaning me for the children's table.

"But not too casual, right? I mean, I want it to be really special tonight. Daniel's brothers have never stepped foot in my house. I don't want them or their wives to think I'm poor white trash."

"They won't. You aren't," BeBe said, gazing down at the card table I'd set up for Daniel's four nieces and nephews with green Depression glass plates and a centerpiece of green-and-red gumdrop trees.

"This is cute," she said, flicking the edge of the tablecloth, a vintage forties luncheon cloth with a bright poinsettia motif border.

"This was in that box lot of stuff I bought at Trader Bob's," I told her. "The one that had the blue Christmas tree pin." I patted the collar of my cream satin blouse, where the brooch was now securely pinned. "And this," I said, pointing to the frilly white taffeta apron I'd tied over my black silk slacks.

"Something's dinging in the oven," Harry Sorrentino announced as he entered the dining room with a large silver bowl heaped high with boiled shrimp.

"Harry, you're an angel," I said, giving him a quick kiss on the cheek. "Are these your shrimp?"

"Yep," Harry said, blushing a little.

"Our shrimp," BeBe corrected. "You may have caught the little buggers, but I'm the one who headed 'em, deveined 'em, and marinated them in the lemon juice and capers."

"But it was my recipe," Harry countered.

Before the good-natured bickering could continue, I heard the key turn in the front door and Daniel stepped inside carrying a foil-wrapped platter.

"Thank God," I breathed, hurrying to take the ham out of his arms. "It's past seven. I was halfway afraid you were going to be a no-show."

He followed me into the kitchen, closing the door behind us.

I made room for the platter on the kitchen table and popped the foil off the ham, which smelled heavenly, with its dark brown maple-sugar-and-orange glaze. He'd even sliced the ham at the restaurant and garnished the platter with gorgeous clusters of sugared grapes.

"It's amazing," I said, kissing him gratefully. "You're forgiven for being late. Now get out of that jacket and give me a hand with the rest of this stuff."

He stepped out of my embrace and looked away.

"What?" I said, knowing in my gut what he was about to say.

"I can't stay," he said. "Eddie's car got T-boned on Eisenhower this afternoon. He's in the hospital."

"Oh no," I said, alarmed. Eddie Gonzalez was Daniel's

best line cook. He'd worked at Guale since the beginning. "Is he going to be all right?"

"Couple broken ribs and some cuts on his face," Daniel said. "But in the meantime, we're swamped. I gotta get back. Forgive me?"

I shrugged. This was the restaurant life, I knew, although I couldn't help but wonder if a part of Daniel wasn't glad to be missing out on this family dinner which he'd only reluctantly agreed to.

"Go," I said, shooing him out of the kitchen.

He gave me a grateful kiss. "I'll call you," he promised. "Maybe things will slacken up a little after nine."

We both knew that was wishful thinking.

I was lifting a bubbling earthenware dish of hot crab dip from the still-dinging oven when Mama and Daddy came in through the back door.

"Merry, merry," Mama chirped, holding out a gaudy green plastic tray.

"I made your favorite," she said.

Gingerly I lifted the edge of the linen napkin covering the tray to view something brown and vaguely cinnamon scented.

"Yum," I said, trying to sound enthusiastic.

"Zucchini bread," Daddy said glumly. "Here I thought she'd given it all away last summer, but there was still one last loaf on the bottom shelf of the freezer."

"Luckily," Mama said.

"Where's Danny?" Daddy asked, making me cringe involuntarily.

"You just missed him," I said lightly. "He brought the ham, then he had to dash back to the restaurant. They're booked solid tonight, and his best cook got in a car accident today."

Mama took her coat off and handed it to Daddy. "Never mind," she said. "Just put me to work instead," she ordered, rolling up the cuffs of her Christmas sweater.

"Oh no," I said quickly. "Out to the living room with the both of you." I gave them a little shove. "I've got my staff helping tonight. You and Daddy are strictly company. I forbid you to lift a finger."

From behind Mama's back, Daddy shot me a grateful wink.

"Come on, Marian," he said, taking her arm. "The front doorbell is ringing. You and I will be official greeters. Is that okay, Weezie?"

"Perfect," I said. I handed Daddy a tray with the crab dip and a basket of Triscuits. "And you can also pass this around and get everybody's drink orders when they come in."

"Just ginger ale for me," Mama said quickly.

"And cranberry juice," I agreed. "To make it look festive."

From the direction of the living room, I heard BeBe greeting our guests, and recognized James's and Jonathan's voices. Then the doorbell rang, and I heard more voices. Daniel's family. I untied my apron, put on some fresh lipstick, and went out to the living room to witness the meeting of the families.

"Well, hello strangers," I said, swooping down on Derek and Sondra, who were standing in the middle of the living room, still wearing their coats, with Sondra clutching a plastic-wrapped casserole dish. I introduced them around, and Harry, bless him, took their coats and fixed them drinks.

"Daniel sends his regrets," I announced before anybody else could ask. "He's hoping to make it back here before dessert, if things slow down at the restaurant."

"Where are the children?" I asked, giving Derek a quick hug.

Sondra blinked. "Children? You mean Sarah Jo and Hollis? They're at my mother's house. They always spend Christmas Eve with their cousins there."

"But look who we did bring!" Derek said, reaching into the huge tote bag on Sondra's shoulder and bringing out the tiniest, most rodentlike animal I'd ever seen.

"Say hello, Barkley," he instructed, rubbing his nose against the animal's snout.

The dog's ears lay flat against his skull and he bared his little fangs and lunged in my direction.

"Rowrowrowrowrow."

"Jesus!" I cried, jumping about a foot in the air.

"Barkley!" Sondra said. She shook a finger at the animal. "That was naughty, naughty."

She laughed apologetically. "Barkley didn't mean it. Our vet says he's overcompensating for being the smallest of his litter with inappropriate aggression."

"Derek?" She narrowed her eyes at her husband. "Sweetie, did you give Barkley his meds tonight? You know he doesn't transition well without his Paxil."

"Wait," Derek said. "You mean Barkley gets the Paxil? Uh-oh. I thought he got the Flintstones chewables. I gave the Paxil to Sarah Jo."

"What?" Sondra shrieked.

"Just kidding," Derek said with a chuckle.

The look Sondra gave him would have melted cast iron.

Then the doorbell rang again, and Harry ushered in Eric and Ellen and their two children, Stoney, a seven-year-old who was too busy playing with his Game Boy to say hello, and five-year-old Stormy, who clung to her mother's side like stink on a dog.

Once Ellen saw Sondra, she and Stormy beat a hasty retreat to the den, where Daddy, Jonathan, and Uncle James had already retreated to watch football on television.

"I'll just put the ice cream in your freezer, Weezie," Eric said. "What about this rice? Where do you want Ellen's rice casserole?"

"Just put it on the dining room sideboard, please," I said.

When I turned around, Sondra had moved to the corner of the living room, standing ramrod straight, eyes focused on nothing in particular, still clutching her casserole dish. In her middle thirties, Sondra was thin to the point of emaciation, and had raven black hair and skin so milky pale you could see a fine network of blue veins in her face. Daniel referred to her as Morticia when his brother wasn't around.

"Here," Mama said, taking Sondra's dinner contribution. "I'll take this into the dining room. Mmm," she enthused. "It smells wonderful. What is it?"

"Tofurkey," Sondra said shyly.

"Oh." Mama's smile dimmed somewhat. "I don't believe I've ever eaten tofurkey before."

"You'll love it," Derek said, putting an affectionate arm

around his wife's shoulder. "Sondra is an amazing cook. You should taste her lentil cakes."

Eric returned to the living room, with two beer bottles in hand, one of which he handed to Derek.

"Yessir," Eric drawled. "Ol' Sondra here whomps up a mean tofu stew. I was just saying to Ellen on the way over here tonight, 'I hope ol' Sondra brings some of that make-believe meat of hers.'"

"Can it, Eric," Derek snapped. "You're not half as funny as you think you are."

"Hey," I said brightly. "Daddy and the other guys are watching the ball game in the den. Want to join them?"

Mama had somehow enticed Sondra to sit on the sofa beside Miss Sudie and BeBe, and I noticed with relief that they seemed to be having a pleasant conversation.

Just then Harry sauntered into the kitchen to get a beer.

"How's it going in the den?" I asked. "Is everybody behaving themselves?"

He popped the cap on a Heineken, took a long swig, and considered the question.

"So far so good, mostly," he said. "They're all hunkered down around Derek's videotape of the 1980 Georgia-Florida game. You know, their championship season. But at halftime I did overhear Eric telling a fag joke to your uncle James."

"Oh no." I moaned, covering my eyes with my hands.

"James was pretty cool about it," Harry said.

There was a scratching at the back door, and Harry went over and looked out. "Hey, Jethro, buddy," he called, opening the door.

"Wait!" I started. "He can't—"

But it was too late. Jethro bounded into the kitchen, delighted to be invited to the party, and hearing voices coming from the living room, he dashed off in that direction.

"Oh no. You'll have to help me catch him now. He can't stay in the house. There are too many people. And Sondra and Derek brought this little dog Jethro could swallow whole in one bite."

"Rowrowrowrow," I heard. We ran into the living room in time to see Jethro, on his haunches, backing away in terror from the attack midget hanging out of Sondra's tote bag, which she'd set on the floor beside her chair.

"Jethro! Here!" I called.

He turned, gave me a reproachful look, and retreated to his favorite hiding place, under the coffee table.

"Rowrowrowrow." Barkley was out of the tote bag, his ears twitching in indignation at this new interloper.

"Here, Jethro," Harry called, getting down on his hands and knees. "Come here, buddy. Come see Uncle Harry."

But instead of going to Harry, Jethro scooted out the other side of the coffee table, where he spied the hot crab dip on top of the table.

He was on it in a flash, wolfing down the entire contents of the bowl before anybody could stop him.

"Jethro! Bad!" I hollered.

He gave me that reproachful look again, and trotted off in the direction of the den.

"I'll get him," Harry volunteered.

"Sorry about the dip," I told the womenfolk. "But dinner's

almost ready anyway, and now you won't spoil your appetites."

"Well, I believe I'll just go out to the kitchen and help you get dinner on the table," Mama said, getting to her feet.

"Owowowow!" Barkley yelped.

"You stood on his tail!" Sondra cried, snatching the dog into her arms.

"Owwooooo," Barkley howled.

"Poor baby," Sondra cooed, cradling the dog in her arms. "Poor angel."

"So sorry," Mama said. "I didn't even see him there."

"You could have killed him!" Sondra said.

BeBe and I followed Mama into the kitchen.

"I should have killed him," Mama muttered. "Who brings a dog to a dinner party?"

"For that matter, who brings tofurkey?" BeBe chimed in.

I was transferring the real turkey to a serving platter when I heard a screech coming from the den.

"Good Lord!" Mama said. "What now?"

"I'll take care of it," I said, hurrying away. "Everything's ready to go out to the sideboard. Except the gravy. Let's leave it on the stove until everybody's seated."

In the den I found the men huddled tensely around the television, watching a twenty-six-year-old football game whose outcome was already etched in their brains. A glance at the screen told the tale—Georgia was trailing Florida 21–20. They were all on their knees, all except Eric. He and Ellen were trying in vain to quiet Stormy's sobs.

"What happened?" I asked.

"Your dog!" Eric shouted at me. "Your goddamned dog—"

Jethro cowered in the corner.

"He bit her?" I asked in disbelief. "Jethro's never bitten anybody in his life."

Wait. Suddenly I smelled it. A hideous, disgusting smell.

"No!" Eric said. "He puked all over my kid's shoes."

"Her brand-new patent leather Stride Rites," Ellen said, her lips tight.

"My shoeeeeees!" Stormy howled.

My crab dip, I wanted to cry.

For the first time, Derek turned away from the television to address his tear-stricken niece.

"Stormy, honey," he said kindly. "It's fourth down and there's less than two minutes left in the game. Buck Belue's fixin' to throw that tater to ol' Lindsay Scott, and your uncle Derek wants to hear Larry Munson scream 'Run, Lindsay, run,' but we can't do that until you shut the fuck up."

"Derek!" Ellen screeched, clamping her hands over her daughter's ears.

"My shoeeees," Stormy wailed.

I sighed and held out my hand to the child. "Come on, Stormy," I said. "Let's go upstairs and get you washed off. I'm sorry about your shoes. I'll buy you a new pair."

"I'll buy her a fuckin' pony if you get her out of here right this minute," Derek called over his shoulder.

CHAPTER 20

At nine o'clock, finally, we all gathered in the dining room, holding hands, seated around the tables.

"Uncle James," I said, nodding in his direction. "Would you ask the blessing?"

Big mistake. Never, ever ask a former clergyman to say the blessing over a holiday dinner. Not if you like your dinner warm, anyway.

Beaming, James started out strong. "Lord," he said earnestly, "we thank you for bringing these two families together tonight. We thank you for the opportunity to remember the reason for this season."

And he went on like that for the next ten minutes. It was a most un-Catholic-like prayer, especially coming from a former priest. James thanked God for the turkey, the ham, the oysters, and the final score of the 1980 Georgia-Florida game. All this time, Daddy was gripping my right hand so tightly that it had gotten totally numb. BeBe, on my right, was giggling silently, her shoulders heaving from the strain of near hilarity. Stoney, at the far end of the children's table, was staring intently at the Game Boy on his lap.

When he slowed down a little, Jonathan jumped in. "And thank you for everything else. Amen!"

"Amen!" the others said in unison, sitting down and looking at me expectantly.

I went to the sideboard and started passing around the bread and cranberry relish.

"Hey," Eric said as I was leaning over to serve him. He reached out and touched the pin on my blouse. "Hey, Derek, did you see Weezie's pin?"

"I noticed that," Derek said. "It's just like the one we bought Mama for Christmas that year."

"I know," I said quietly. "Daniel told me the whole story about how you boys used all your lawn-mowing money to buy it for her."

"*We* didn't all buy it," Eric corrected me. "Daniel and I pooled our money. But hotshot over there," he said, pointing to Derek, "spent all his money buying an ankle bracelet for his girlfriend."

"Oh yeah." Derek grinned. "I remember the bracelet, but I can't for the life of me remember that little ol' gal's name."

"Hmmph," Sondra said, glaring at him.

"I can't remember her real name either," Eric said mischievously. "Only her nickname. Huffy."

"Huffy?" Ellen wrinkled her nose in distaste. "What kind of nickname is that?"

"Never mind," Derek said quickly. "Forget it. Ancient history."

"No, really," Ellen persisted.

"We called her Huffy," Eric said, guffawing now, "cuz every guy on our block took a ride on her."

"Eric!" Ellen said, blushing beet red. "There are children in the room. Our children."

"That's revolting," Sondra said.

"Thanks, bro," Derek said under his breath. "I owe you one."

"Who's ready for turkey?" I called, escaping into the kitchen.

That turkey was a thing of beauty. I'd soaked it overnight in a salt and herb brine, stuffed it with roast chestnuts and wild rice, tucked more herbs and butter and garlic under the skin, and basted it all morning with an apple cider glaze.

It was golden and regal, resting on my best Staffordshire platter on top of a bed of roasted potatoes, parsnips, carrots, and onions.

I set the platter down on the table with a flourish. "Daddy? Daniel usually carves the meat, but he's still stuck at the restaurant. Do you feel like carving tonight?"

"Oh no," Mama interjected. "Your father is terrible at carving. Ask somebody else."

Daddy glowered at her, but kept silent.

"I'll give it a shot," Eric volunteered. "I was the oldest in our family, so Mama always let me carve all the meat. I'm pretty good at it too."

"He really is," Ellen agreed. "He watches all those cooking

shows on FoodTV." She beamed at her husband, then reached into her lap and brought out a small plastic bottle of clear liquid. I watched, fascinated, as she squirted the liquid into her hands and rubbed them together briskly.

"What's that?" Mama asked. "Hand lotion?"

"Oh no," Ellen said. "Just Purell. It's a disinfectant." She called Stormy over, and the little girl held out her hands to be squirted. Stoney, unprompted, came over and held out his hands for his dose.

I watched, stunned, as she proceeded to polish my wedding silver with the contents of another plastic bottle that appeared from nowhere.

Ellen caught me staring.

"No offense," she said. "But you never know what kind of food-borne pathogens are lurking in the average American household. Poultry, especially, is vulnerable to a whole host of opportunistic bacteria. You've got your salmonella, your botulism, and of course, if the food's been prepared in anything less than totally hygienic conditions, you run the risk of cryptosporidium."

Everybody at the table suddenly put down their forks and looked at me expectantly.

"My kitchen is clean," I cried. "I always wash my hands."

Ellen shook her head sadly. "Unless you scrub under hot water for at least three minutes with an antibacterial soap, you're just inviting trouble."

Eric rolled his eyes. "Shut up, Ellen," he said. "I'm sure crypto-whatever is not on Weezie's menu tonight."

He picked up my stag-handled carving set and plunged the knife into the turkey breast.

"There's a real science to carving a bird like this," he began. "I like to start with the breast, putting the knife on the diagonal, like this."

As we watched, paper-thin slices of white meat fell obligingly onto the platter. The irresistible smell of roasted meat filled the room. People picked up their forks again. They sipped wine and passed vegetables. It was going well. I congratulated myself.

And then it happened.

Eric was demonstrating how he liked to separate the whole leg from the turkey carcass. He made an extravagant cut into the bird, then cried out.

"Oh shit!"

He held up his left hand. The tip of his pinkie dangled by a strand of flesh. Blood spurted onto his white shirtfront.

"Oh shit," he repeated, sinking down into his chair. Blood poured from his hand as he stared dumbly down at the spreading crimson pool on the turkey platter and the table.

"Here," James said, jumping up and running over to him. He grabbed Eric's hand and wrapped it in a damask napkin. "Keep the pressure on it," he said calmly.

"Eric!" Ellen cried. Her face went white and she slumped forward in her chair, striking her head on her dinner plate, and cracking it neatly in two pieces.

"Mama!" Stormy screamed. "My mama is dead!"

"Call an ambulance," Sondra cried. "My God, now she's bleeding too."

Eric tilted his head against his chair back. "No ambulance," he said weakly. "My insurance won't pay for an ambulance."

"Mama," Stormy wailed.

BeBe knelt beside Ellen, holding another napkin to a nasty gash in her forehead.

She looked up at me. "I'm no expert, but I think she's gonna need stitches."

"For God's sake." Derek jumped up out of his chair. "Come on then," he said. "Harry, can you help me carry Ellen out to my car? James, you and Jonathan get Eric. We'll take 'em both over to the ER at Memorial."

Sondra stood up too. "Why can't you take Eric's truck?" she said plaintively. "We just had your car detailed."

"Give me the keys," Derek ordered, holding out his hand.

"I want my mama," Stormy howled, latching onto Derek's knees. "Don't take my mama away."

"Stormy, honey," Derek said, leaning down and tenderly brushing away the tears streaming down the little girl's face. "Shut the fuck up."

CHAPTER 21

"Weezie, wake up!"

I opened my eyes slowly. Daniel was kneeling down beside the sofa, still in his grease-stained chef's smock. His thick hair was more rumpled than ever, and there were dark circles of fatigue under his eyes.

I yawned, sat up, and looked around. Had I dreamed this calamitous evening? One look at the living room told me that my nightmare was reality. The place was a wreck. Beer cans and wineglasses littered the tabletops, and a blood-soaked napkin had been discarded on the floor by the sofa where I'd fallen into a catatonic sleep after the untimely departure of my dinner guests.

"What happened here? Where is everybody?" Daniel asked.

"Where were you? I tried and tried to call you, but I never got any answer."

"Sorry," he said sheepishly. "The restaurant was a mad-house. I forgot and left my cell phone on the front seat of the truck. I only saw how many calls I'd missed after I locked up for the night."

He reached over and ruffled my hair. "I'm really, really sorry about tonight. Swear to God, I tried to get away earlier. Besides Eddie being out, half my waitstaff didn't show up for work either. I'm gonna kick some major ass come Tuesday. Just when it started to slow down, there were two parties of twelve apiece who decided to linger over coffee and dessert so long that I eventually had to come out of the kitchen and politely start stacking chairs on tables myself."

I sighed. I could have bitched him out, or given him the silent treatment, but that wouldn't solve anything. Owning a restaurant, in particular a successful one like Guale, meant hard work and long hours—especially on the holidays.

"It's okay," I said finally. "After all, you did give me fair warning about your family."

He put an arm around my shoulders and drew me closer. "What in God's name went on here tonight? Was there some kind of knife fight? There's a trail of blood leading from the street into the dining room. When I pulled up out front and saw the blood, I halfway expected to find you all dead or maimed in here."

I took a deep breath. "Where should I start? It's been a long, hairy night."

"Whose blood?" he asked, examining my arms for wounds.

"Oh, yeah," I said. "That would be the blood of your

brother Eric. He was demonstrating his prowess in turkey carving and managed to slice off the tip of his pinkie."

"Jesus!" Daniel said.

"That's what I said too. There was quite a bit of blood, as you could imagine. Then, when Ellen saw Eric's finger, she passed out cold—hitting her head on her dinner plate and splitting her forehead wide open. Not to mention breaking one of my hundred-fifty-dollar flow blue plates."

"I'll buy you a new plate," Daniel said. "What else?"

"Well, when little Stormy saw both her mama and her daddy bleeding like stuck pigs and being hauled off to the emergency room by her uncle Derek, she went into uncontrollable hysterics. We finally had to dose her up with some of Sondra's dog's Paxil."

"You gave doggy downers to my niece?" Daniel asked. "Was that wise?"

"It shut her up, and that's all we cared about at the time," I said.

Daniel buried his head in his hands. Suddenly I saw his shoulders quaking with emotion. I patted his back soothingly.

"Don't worry. Everybody's all right. James went to the hospital with them. They managed to reattach Eric's fingertip, and they got Ellen's forehead stitched up by the town's best plastic surgeon, whose mom happens to play bridge with Miss Sudie. Stormy's fine too, although they expect her to sleep till noon tomorrow."

Daniel lifted his head. Tears streamed down his face, and I realized he was actually choking on his own peals of laughter.

"I'm sorry," he said, gasping. "It's not really funny—but then again, in a really sick way, it is funny."

He kissed me. "Someday we'll look back on this night and laugh about it. But I do regret that you had to endure it all by yourself."

"At least BeBe and Harry were here," I said. "After the family cleared out, they helped me clean up the kitchen. And anyway, it's not like my family was entirely blameless."

"Don't tell me your mother took a drink," Daniel said.

"No, thank God. But she did step on Sondra's dog and almost killed it. And then Jethro ate the crab dip and puked all over Stormy's shoes. Also Mama caught Daddy feeding her famous zucchini bread to Barkley, Sondra's dog, and she got furious and demanded to be taken home."

Daniel was wheezing he was laughing so hard.

"What happened to your beautiful dinner? Did anybody get to eat?"

"No," I said succinctly. "Oddly enough, everybody's appetite was somewhat dimmed by the appearance of a turkey drenched in human blood. They cleared out of here so fast it made my head spin."

Daniel's face fell. "No turkey sandwiches? No turkey hash?"

"I pitched it in the garbage. There's plenty of ham, of course, and some oyster dressing in the fridge, and some veggies too. I'd offer you some of your sister-in-law's tofurkey, but she took it with her when she left."

"Tofurkey, phooey," Daniel said. He stood up and pulled me to my feet.

"There's still all that dessert—right? I didn't have time to eat tonight. I'm starved. Come on, let's go raid the fridge."

"There's still a lot of dessert left," I said. "But you can forget about the pumpkin pie."

"What happened to the pumpkin pie? You know it's my favorite."

"Stoney Stipanek happened to it. In the rush to get Eric and Ellen to the hospital, everybody forgot about little Stoney. I forgot about him myself until I went into the den to turn off the Christmas tree lights. He was sound asleep on the sofa, his damned Game Boy clutched in one hand and the empty pumpkin pie pan in the other."

"Pie-eating pig," Daniel muttered. "Just like his old man. When we were kids, Eric used to sneak back into the kitchen after everybody had gone to bed, and he'd eat every sweet in sight. One time he ate a whole can of Hershey's chocolate syrup. Kid weighed two hundred pounds in the fifth grade."

"You'd never guess that now," I commented. "Eric's thinner than you or Derek."

"You'd be thin too if you had to eat a steady diet of Ellen's cooking," Daniel told me, slicing himself a thick slab of pecan pie. "So where's Stoney now?"

"Home. Derek came back and fetched him."

His mouth full, Daniel nodded approval. "Good. You got any milk?"

"Soy milk," I said with a grin. "Sondra's contribution, natch. The kids drank all my real milk while the grown-ups were sniping at each other and watching the football game."

"Beer?"

"If your brothers and Harry didn't drink it all."

He was rooting around in my fridge for more food when the doorbell rang.

Daniel looked at the clock on the kitchen wall. "It's past eleven. You got any other family members expected for dinner tonight?"

"None," I promised. "Stay here and I'll get rid of whoever it is."

A Savannah police officer stood on my doorstep, his hand clamped firmly around the arm of a petite old lady dressed in a maroon BC letter sweater.

"Annie!" I exclaimed.

"Ma'am?" the cop said, looking from me to Annie. "I just apprehended this here suspect trying to break into a green pickup truck parked out here at the curb. She claims she knows you."

"She does," I said quickly. "And she wasn't really breaking in. She was picking up a gift I left for her."

"See?" Annie snapped at the cop. "What'd I tell you?"

The cop looked dubious. "You're leaving gifts in your truck for a bag lady? Ma'am, there's a lot of crime downtown. You don't want to be leaving your truck unlocked. These street people will steal you blind."

"Hey!" Annie said, squirming furiously. "I'm no bag lady. You see any shopping bags hanging off of me? You see me pushing a Kroger grocery cart?"

"She's a friend," I assured the cop. "Leave her with me. I'll personally vouch for her."

"All right," he said, obviously reluctant to relinquish his prisoner. "I'm releasing her to your custody."

The temperature was dropping, and an icy wind whipped down the street. "Come on in," I said, gently tugging at Annie's arm. "It's freezing outside."

"Hey!" Annie said, backpedaling as fast as she could. "Don't leave me here, officer. Go ahead, arrest me. I'll go quietly."

"One more thing," the cop added. He reached in his jacket pocket and brought out a small, bedraggled-looking teddy bear. "She had this too. I figure it's yours."

I looked from Annie to the cop. "Thank you," I said. "Merry Christmas." And then I closed and locked the door.

Annie looked wildly around the room, like a caged animal. "I've got to go," she said in a low voice. "Just let me leave, all right? No harm done. We both know you left that bag for me. That stupid cop wouldn't believe me. I tried to tell him—"

"Hey, Weezie," Daniel called, strolling into the living room, "who was at the door?"

Annie's face turned ghost white. She reached for the doorknob, but I reached it first.

"Don't go," I said softly. "I've been worried sick about you for the past two days. Come on. Stay. It's Christmas Eve. We were just going to have some dessert. I know you like sweets."

"No! I can't. Gotta go," she stammered. "I won't bother you again. Please?"

Daniel put his plate of cake on the console table by the door. "Who's this?"

I looked from Daniel to Annie and back again. Her hair was salt-and-pepper, with more salt than anything else, but it was still dense and wavy, and her eyebrows, thick for a woman, were set above very blue, very frightened eyes.

"BeBe and I have been calling her Apple Annie," I said apologetically. "I didn't know her real name. Not till just now."

"And?" Daniel said impatiently. "What is her real name? And what's she doing at your house on Christmas Eve? I swear, Weezie, you are a magnet for weirdness—"

And then he saw the teddy bear in my hand. Wordlessly, he took it from me.

"Where did this come from?"

I nodded in Annie's direction. "She brought it here," I said.

A single tear floated down the old woman's haunted face.

"You're Paula, right?" I asked. "Paula Stipanek."

She tried furiously to blink the tears away. "Not Stipanek. Not anymore. It's Paula Gambrell."

"Welcome home, Paula," I said. "I'd introduce you to the rest of your family too, but they had to leave early. I'm afraid it's just me and you. And your son."

"Danny." She whispered the name. "Oh, God. I should never have come back."

CHAPTER 22

Is this some kind of joke?" Daniel asked, his face ashen under the shock of hair that had fallen in his eye. "Are you for real?"

The old lady reached out and touched his hand, but he jerked away from her. "Danny?"

"I'll leave you two alone," I said, heading for the kitchen. "Coffee. I'll make some coffee. And, Annie, I mean, Paula, would you like some dessert? I've got cake and pie—"

Daniel grabbed my hand. "Stay." Then his face softened, and he gave my hand a gentle squeeze. "Please?"

"Only if it's okay with your mom," I said, glancing over at Paula.

She peeled off the BC letter sweater and thrust it at me. "Here. I'm sorry. I shouldn't have taken it. I shouldn't have come here and bothered you at all. I'll just go. All right?"

She was edging back toward the front door.

"Do what you want," Daniel said, looking down at the teddy bear. "But tell me something, what's this supposed to mean? Why did you come back after all this time? Why now?"

The old lady's eyes filled with tears again. "I've been back in Savannah for a couple months now. I came . . . I guess I came back because I had nowhere else to go."

She stared down at the floor. "Hoyt. My husband? He died in September. He'd been sick for a long time, ever since he went to prison. Heart disease."

"I'm so sorry," I said as I perched on the arm of the sofa. "Please, won't you sit down? And let me fix you something to eat and drink?"

"I'm really not hungry," Paula said with a sad smile. "We had a feast at the Salvation Army tonight. Ham and collard greens and mashed potatoes and pumpkin pie, and eggnog, without the whiskey, of course."

"I still don't understand what you're doing here," Daniel said, his jaw set in a hard, unforgiving line.

Paula shrugged. "I'm not sure I understand myself. I guess I needed to make sure you were all right."

"I'm fine," he snapped. "Anyway, you're a day late and a dollar short."

"Daniel!" I punched his arm angrily. "If you can't be polite, you can leave. This is my home and your mother is a guest of mine."

Paula sat uneasily on the edge of the armchair nearest the door. "I don't blame you for feeling the way you do about me. I feel that way about myself. Worse, maybe, if that's possible."

"You don't know anything about how I feel about you

walking away and leaving us," Daniel said. "Leaving us for him. I felt something years ago. But I don't now. I don't feel one way or another about you."

"I wouldn't expect you to feel any differently," Paula said. Her hands were folded neatly in her lap. "But that doesn't stop me from caring about you. From worrying about you and your life. And your brothers."

"That's just a pile of crap," Daniel said angrily. "I don't want to hear any more."

Now he was the one who was standing up and walking toward the door.

"Dammit!" I said fiercely, grabbing his arm. "Just stay. Hear what she has to say."

He sank back down onto the sofa, crossing his arms across his chest. "I'm listening."

Paula's face softened and she almost smiled. "You used to do that when you were a little boy. You were the most mule-headed child I'd ever seen. If you didn't get what you wanted, you'd stick out that chin and cross your arms and just dig in your heels. People said you got that from me."

Daniel stared at the ceiling.

"I never meant to leave you for good," Paula said. "After Hoyt went to prison, I thought, well, I thought I'd send for you boys after things settled down. But there was no money. I was living in a tiny little apartment not far from the prison down in Jacksonville, waitressing in a coffee shop, working nights. Eventually, after a year or so, I did come back to Savannah. I meant to take you all back to Jacksonville with me. I'd been saving up to get a larger place, and I figured

Derek was old enough then, he could look after you younger boys while I worked."

"You came back?" Daniel seemed surprised. "Nobody ever told us."

"Nobody knew," Paula said. "Your aunt was furious with me for leaving. I didn't dare call her or come around the house while you were staying with her. I just kind of snuck into town. I rode past the house, and I actually saw you and Eric outside, shooting basketball at that hoop she'd tacked up on the garage. And you looked happy, you know? I drove past your school, and I watched Derek's football practice. I just . . . didn't have the heart to uproot you. You boys were settled in school, you had your friends, and your aunt. I couldn't ask you to make that move."

"You could have given us the option of deciding for ourselves," Daniel said, his voice icy. "Instead of playing the martyr."

"I was a coward," Paula said, sitting up very straight. "There'd been that big scandal, when Hoyt was arrested, and then the trial. It was so ugly. Everybody thought I was trash. I thought so too. And I thought, if I weren't around, eventually people would forget that I was your mother. Then . . . the longer I stayed away, the harder it seemed I could ever get my boys back."

"We did all right for ourselves," Daniel said. "All three of us. Despite what you did to us."

"You did more than all right," Paula said eagerly. Her face was glowing now. "I've seen the restaurant, how successful it is. And the children, Eric's and Derek's, so beautiful. A friend here loans me a car sometimes, and I drive past their houses. I snuck into Stormy's dance recital last month." She sighed. "What I wouldn't give to hold those precious babies."

"You still can," I said, ignoring Daniel's icy glare. "The past is past. I bet if Eric and Derek talked to you, if they heard your side of things, they'd want to see you. Want you to get to know your grandchildren."

"No," Paula said hastily. "I don't have that right. Seeing them is enough for now."

"Paula? Can I ask you something?"

"Sure."

"Were you the one who broke into this house—and ate the appetizers?"

She blushed and nodded. "I didn't really break in. You left a set of keys on the seat of your truck one night. I took them so nobody else would. There's a lot of crime downtown, you know."

"I do now," I said, laughing.

"I ran off those street bums after they picked all the fruit off your beautiful decorations that night," she said proudly.

"If they were really hungry, they were welcome to the fruit."

"And I want to apologize about taking your goodies," Paula said. "I didn't realize you were having a party that night. I shared it with the girls over at the Salvation. They'd never seen such grand food in their lives."

"It's all right," I said. "As it turns out, there was plenty of food for everybody."

"And Jethro?" I asked. "You found him and brought him home?"

She nodded. "He was way down on River Street, rummaging through some garbage cans in back of one of the bars down there. He's a sweet old thing, isn't he? He came along just as nice as you please, once I tied that rope to his collar."

"So—" Daniel cut in. "You've been watching us? Me and Weezie? Why?"

"I was worried about you," she said simply. "Your brothers, they're settled down. Got nice wives and children and homes. And this young lady"—she gestured toward me—"you've been keeping her steady company."

Now it was my turn to blush.

"We'll settle down," Daniel said. "When the time is right."

"What makes you think the time is ever right?" Paula said. "You think God cares about your plans? I thought I'd have all the time in the world with your daddy. But I was wrong. About that and a lot of other things."

Daniel gave a derisive snort.

"Do you love her, son?"

His face darkened. "That's between us."

"Just answer, please. As a favor to an old lady."

He reached over and took my hand. "I've loved her since I was eighteen years old."

Paula nodded at me. "And you?"

I smiled and nodded. "He kind of grows on you, doesn't he?"

"He was an ornery baby," she said. "Beautiful, but ornery."

"Still is," I agreed. "Paula, where have you been the past

few days? When you didn't pick up your present, I was really worried."

"Present?" Daniel asked.

"Your mother and I have been exchanging Christmas gifts for the past few days," I said. "She gave me some wonderful gifts. A room key to the old DeSoto Hotel. A tiny seashell. A gorgeous blue John Ryan bottle. And this," I said, touching the Christmas tree brooch pinned to my collar.

"But you bought that pin. At the auction," Daniel said. "And she stole it."

"Borrowed it," Paula and I said at the exact same time.

"And I gave it back," Paula added. "Weezie's given me gifts too." She held up the red plaid gift bag. "First gifts anybody's given me in years."

"But where have you been?" I asked.

"Jacksonville," Paula said. "I took the bus back down to Jacksonville. I was going to stay down there too. I'd seen about my boys. They were doing just fine. Even Daniel."

"Then why come back?" Daniel challenged.

"I had all my things in storage, in the prison chaplain's basement," Paula said. "Not that there was very much. I've learned to live lean since Hoyt died. I was going through my things, and I found that," she said, pointing at the bear. "And I wanted you to have it, son."

"Old bear," Daniel said, holding the tattered stuffed animal in both hands. "I'd forgotten about him."

"You slept with him until you were six, and your brothers teased you so for being a baby, you threw it in the trash,"

Paula said. "I rescued him, and I've been saving him all this time. Do you remember the song he plays?"

Daniel turned the bear over and wound a key protruding from his back.

"Teddy bear," he said as the tinkling mechanical tune began. "Just wanna be your teddy bear."

"Elvis again?" I asked.

"Yes, ma'am," Paula said proudly. "I was always a huge Elvis fan. I was at his last concert here in Savannah, February 1977, right here at the Civic Center, last one he gave here before he died."

"I like Elvis too," I said. "Always have."

"Danny here was named for a character Elvis played in a movie. Did you know that, son?"

"You're kidding."

"No sir. You were named for the boy in *King Creole*. Best movie he ever made."

"I love that!" I said gleefully.

"Nobody calls me Danny anymore," he said accusingly.

"I do. Sometimes," I said.

"You're a gal who appreciates the good things," Paula said approvingly. "Like that pin."

I touched the Christmas tree brooch. "It's not . . . the same one, is it? The one your boys gave you?"

"See for yourself," she said, reaching into the pocket of her worn brown slacks. She held her hand out, palm open for us to see. In it was another blue Christmas tree pin. Not exactly the same as mine, but close.

"That was the real reason I went back to Jacksonville,"

Paula said. "To see if I could find that pin. When I did, I started to think. What could happen if I came back to Savannah? Could I make a difference to my boys?"

We both looked expectantly at Daniel.

"He hates Christmas," I told Paula. "That's how I got the idea for the Blue Christmas theme for the antiques shop."

Daniel shook his head. "She probably hates it too. Seems like everything bad always happens around the holidays."

"Not everything," Paula said. "Sometimes good things happen. Sometimes, if you work at it, you can find what you lost at Christmas."

I heard a faint scratching from the front door.

"The cops again?" Daniel said.

When I opened the front door to investigate, I was assaulted by a blast of freezing air and a small, wet bundle of black fur that shot inside the door.

At the same time, Jethro, who'd been asleep under the coffee table, raised his snout, took one look, and leaped to his feet.

"What the hell?" Daniel said as the black dog raced past him into the kitchen, followed by Jethro.

"That's Ruthie," I said, peeking into the kitchen, where the two dogs were crouched side by side over Jethro's food bowl. "She belongs to Manny and Cookie. You know, the guys across the square who own Babalu. She must have gotten loose. I guess I better take her home. She's their little princess. They'll probably assume she's been dognapped."

"Stray dogs and bag ladies," Daniel said, shaking his head. "The joys of living downtown."

"I am *not* a bag lady," Paula said indignantly. She picked up her gift and buttoned the cardigan she'd been wearing under the letter sweater. "I'll be glad to take Ruthie home," she volunteered. "I know right where she lives."

"What about later, Paula?" I asked. "Where will you stay tonight?"

She shrugged. "Not at the Salvation, thanks to that cop who hauled me in here. They lock the doors at eleven sharp. Nobody gets in after that. But don't worry about me. I'll find a place. I always do."

I shot Daniel a helpless look.

"You can't sleep on the streets," he said gruffly. "It's freezing out there. And from the looks of that dog, it's starting to rain too. Come on. I'll drop you at a motel."

"I can't."

"It's on me," Daniel said. "Christmas present."

Just then the doorbell rang. The three of us turned to stare at it.

"Now what?" Daniel muttered.

CHAPTER 23

This time my guests were human.

Manny and Cookie, dressed in soaking-wet formal wear, stood huddled together on my doorstep, rain streaking down their faces.

"Ruthie's gone," Manny blurted. "We just got back from candlelight services at the Cathedral. I don't know how she got out—"

"She'll freeze to death," Cookie cut in. "She's not used to being out without a jacket—"

"We had a workman in, dealing with the hot water heater, and he must have left the back gate open," Manny said. "We don't know how long she's been out—"

"She's here," I said quickly. "In the kitchen, sharing Jethro's dinner."

"Thank God," Cookie exclaimed.

I led them into the kitchen, where Jethro and Ruthie were curled up asleep on Jethro's bed, snout to snout.

"My precious!" Manny whispered, tugging at Cookie's sleeve. "Would you look at this? Did you ever?"

"Does this remind you of—"

"Lady and the Tramp!" Manny said. "Forbidden love. And yet—"

"They're very sweet together," Cookie concluded. "I don't even have the heart to wake her up and take her home, she's so warm and cozy."

"She can stay tonight," I offered. "I'll bring her home in the morning."

"What do you think?" Manny asked his partner.

Cookie shrugged. "What's one night? All right. She's already knocked up. So she can stay. Thank you."

"You're welcome," I said, hesitating a moment. "Look. I was just making some coffee. And we've got all this pie left from dinner. Would you like to join us?"

Cookie nudged Manny. "Tell her," he whispered.

"Tell me what?"

"We're sorry," Manny said, twisting the tasseled ends of the white silk scarf tossed casually around his neck. "We haven't been very good neighbors to you. And now that we're practically in-laws, well, we'd like to start over. We got all off on the wrong foot, and acted like pissy little queens. And that is so *not* who we are."

I blushed. "I haven't been very friendly either. The two of you are so creative and talented, I guess I felt threatened by your success with Babalu."

"Us, creative?" Cookie hooted. "Sweetie, lamb, when we saw that Blue Christmas display of yours, we were just knocked for a loop. We have *never*—"

"—seen anything as fabulous!" Manny said with a giggle. "Are you sure you're straight?"

"Positive," Daniel said, walking into the kitchen. "She's definitely straight. I can vouch for that." He leaned down and scratched Ruthie's ear, and she wagged her tail in bliss.

"Daniel," I said, "these are my neighbors. Cookie and Manny."

"Friends," Cookie corrected. "We're your friends."

"And in-laws," Manny added.

"The boys were just going to join us for some coffee and dessert," I said.

"Great," Daniel said.

"So I'll just go drop Paula off at a motel and be right back."

"No motel," I said. "It's Christmas Eve. She stays here tonight."

"May I speak with you in the other room?" Daniel said, his voice tense.

"Your mother is in the other room," I reminded him. "Do you want her to hear us fussing about where she's staying?"

"That's your *mom*?" Cookie asked.

"What about it?" Daniel snapped. "Not that it's any of your business, but she left my brothers and me when we were kids. We were raised by an aunt. Now she waltzes back into town and expects me to feel all warm and fuzzy."

"Oh puh-leeze," Cookie drawled. "My mama beat me with a hairbrush when she caught me waxing my eyebrows in tenth grade. And Daddy still tells people that Manny's my 'business associate.'"

"Hard-shell Baptists, through and through," Manny said

with a sigh. "Neither one of them would set foot at our commitment ceremony," he added. "Although they did send a place setting of our good silver, which was very generous, considering. But so what? They're our family. My folks are dead. So we're stuck with Ma and Pa Parker."

"You don't understand," Daniel said. "There's a lot more to it than that."

"Puh-leeze," Cookie repeated. "Grow up and get over yourself."

I wrapped my arms around Daniel's waist and leaned in close. "One night," I said. "Just let her stay one night. For me."

He kissed the top of my head, which I took as a good sign.

"One night," he repeated. "Just for you. But I have to tell you, this solves nothing."

"Thank you," I whispered. Flushed with good cheer, I went to the living room, to ask Paula what she wanted in her coffee.

She was gone, but my daddy's letter sweater was still draped over the back of the chair where she'd been sitting.

Back in the kitchen, Cookie and Manny were admiring my heart-pine cabinets and Sub-Zero refrigerator, while Daniel poured coffee into the mugs I'd set out.

"Daniel!" I said sharply. "She's gone."

He sighed and set down the coffeepot. "All right. Let me just get my coat and gloves."

"Can I ask you guys a favor?" I asked, turning to my newfound friends.

"Sure," Cookie said. "If you tell me where you found these nickel-plated faucets."

"Deal," I said quickly. "Paula's gone. Daniel and I are going out to look for her. Can you stay here, in case she comes back?"

Manny was lifting the foil from a tray of dessert. "Oh no! Pecan pie," he moaned. "A moment on the lips, a lifetime on the hips."

"Knock yourself out," I said, grabbing the keys to my truck.

CHAPTER 24

The cold and rain seemed to have swept the historic district's streets clean by the time the bells at St. John's and the Lutheran Church of the Ascension tolled midnight.

Daniel drove my truck and I kept my face pressed to the passenger-side window, looking for some glimpse of Paula. Neither of us said much until we'd worked our way all the way north to Bay Street.

"How old do you think she is?" I asked.

"Who?"

"Your mother," I said, exasperated.

"No idea."

"Well, how old is Eric?"

He had to think about it. "Thirty-nine?"

"How old was she when she married your father?"

His face flushed.

"What?" I asked.

"They had to get married, okay? She was a junior and my old man was, like, nineteen. She never even finished high school."

"So she was probably no more than seventeen when she had Eric. My God, Daniel, do you realize your mother isn't even sixty yet?"

"So?" He drummed his fingers impatiently on the steering wheel. "This is useless, Weezie. For all we know, she could have hopped a dog by now to head back to Jacksonville."

"Good idea," I said. "Let's check the Greyhound station."

He turned the car west, toward Martin Luther King Boulevard and the bus depot.

"Paula's not even sixty, but she looks as old or older than my mama, and she's seventy-two," I pointed out.

"Back in the day, my mother was a real knockout," Daniel said. "There was a picture of her in a bathing suit at the beach, standing by the edge of the water, in an old family album. I always assumed the girl in the picture was a movie star until Aunt Lucy told me it was . . . Paula."

We pulled into the bus station parking lot and peered through the brightly lit picture window. We could see a few people standing around, and a maintenance man, pushing a floor-waxing machine. Before Daniel could object, I hopped out of the truck and dashed inside.

Less than five minutes later, I was back, shivering from the rain and cold.

"No luck," I said, trying to catch my breath. "There aren't any buses to Jacksonville tonight. The last one left at eight."

Daniel turned the heater up and pulled away from the curb. "This is hopeless. I'm taking you home before you catch pneumonia."

I didn't dare point out that his mother was out in this weather alone, wearing nothing warmer than a moth-eaten sweater.

"She was just a kid when she had you," I said. "Barely into her twenties. And all of a sudden, after your dad left, she was a single mom with three little boys to take care of."

"Lots of people become single parents at a young age," Daniel said. "They don't abandon their kids when they find a new partner."

"What were you doing when you were in your early twenties?" I asked.

He snorted. "That's different. I was in the Marines. I was partying, raising hell, like every other guy I knew."

"Think about what Paula's life was like," I urged. "Just out of her teens, saddled with three little boys. She's working at the sugar plant, and she meets some smooth-talking boss who sweeps her off her feet—"

He glared at me. "Why are we having this discussion? You don't know anything about her. Anyway, she said it herself. She was a selfish coward."

"It's Christmas," I said, wanting to change the subject. As we rounded the square by the Cathedral of St. John the Baptist, we saw people emerging from the church, umbrellas unfurled like a forest of mushrooms. "And I promised Mama I'd go to mass with her this year."

"Was she mad at you for not going?" he asked.

"No. I think she understood that when dinner went haywire I wasn't going anywhere. She might be disappointed, but not mad."

"No guilt trip?"

I smiled. "Well, maybe a little one."

We were on Charlton Street now, and it pleased me to see the blue glow of my shop windows reflected in the rain-slicked street in front of the shop.

"Hey," I said suddenly. "I've got an idea."

We parked at the curb and walked over to the shop, and stood in the rain to look at Paula Stipanek Gambrell, sound asleep in the display bed.

Daniel slipped an arm out of his jacket and pulled it over my head to shield me from the worst of the weather.

"She doesn't look all that evil," I observed.

"Not even sixty," he said. "But she's been all beat up by life."

Paula's skin looked dark and leathery in the pale wash of lights from the windows, her short-cropped hair dark silver against the white bed linens.

"She's much smaller than I remembered," he said. "And her hair! Look how gray. It used to be jet black. She wore it long, almost to her waist."

He shook his head, and raindrops splattered on my cheek. "She's nothing like I thought she'd be now. Hoyt Gambrell was a rich man before he went away to prison. I always pictured her living on some golf course, playing bridge with a bunch of rich country-club women."

I slid an arm around his waist. "Maybe she did you a favor—leaving you with your aunt. You guys had a home in a decent neighborhood. A middle-class upbringing. She couldn't have given you that."

He clutched me tightly to his chest, and I could hear the even in and out of his breathing. I looked up, and he looked away.

"That last Christmas, before she left? It was the best one we'd ever had. Hoyt must have slipped her some extra money. Derek got an NBA regulation basketball and Eric got a slick skateboard. We all got new clothes and sneakers."

"What about you? What'd you get?"

He laughed. "What I'd been begging for. An Easy-Bake Oven. And a Popeil Pocket Fisherman like I'd seen on television. I was a weird little dude, huh?"

"You were a prodigy," I protested.

"What should we do?" he asked haltingly. "Chase her off? Wake her up and take her back to your place?"

I had a ready answer for that one, but I managed to choke it back. "It's your call."

"Let her sleep," he said finally, steering me toward my own front door. "If she's not gone by morning, we'll figure something out."

"We?"

"Yeah. All of us. My mom. You and me. And my brothers."

The living room was dark when we stepped inside. We found Manny and Cookie in the kitchen, sipping eggnog and giggling like a couple of teenagers.

"Hope you don't mind," Manny said, jumping up to greet us.

"Did you find her?" Cookie asked. "Is she coming back here?"

"She was asleep. At my shop," I said.

"It's late," Daniel said pointedly.

When they'd finally gone, we locked the front and back doors, and checked a final time on the dogs curled up together on Jethro's bed.

"You sleepy?" Daniel asked as I headed toward the stairs.

"Not really," I admitted. "I was tired earlier, but I think I'm too keyed up now to sleep."

"It's officially Christmas," he said, pointing to the clock on the mantel. "Maybe Santa came while we were out."

"The way things have gone around here tonight it's more likely that the Grinch came and shoved all our presents and the roast beast up the chimney while little Cindy Lou Who was asleep," I said. "But we could check."

I reached for the light switch in the darkened den, but Daniel caught my hand. "Let's leave 'em off," he suggested. He went over to the fireplace and switched on the gas logs, then slowly lit the dozen or so candles I'd arranged on the mantel. While he was lighting the candles, I found the remote control switch for the Christmas tree and clicked it on.

When I saw the lit tree, I burst into laughter.

"What's so funny?" Daniel asked, turning abruptly.

"The tree," I said, pointing at the eight-foot Fraser fir.

"It's beautiful," he said, coming to stand beside me. "Prettiest tree you've ever decorated."

"Except I didn't decorate it this way," I told him. "Look at the way those strands of twinkle lights are draped in precise six-inch loops."

"So?"

"So I just threw 'em on there any old way. And where are my big ol' gaudy colored lights? And my tinsel? I had about a ton of tinsel on this tree earlier. And now there's not even a smidge. Not to mention the way the gifts are so artfully arranged under the tree. Look at it! It looks like something out of a magazine."

"I don't get it," Daniel said. "If you didn't do this, who did?"

"A couple of elves named Manny and Cookie."

"Damn," Daniel said.

"I know. We've been the victims of a drive-by redecorate."

"It's still a beautiful tree," he said, his dark blue eyes suddenly serious. "Perfect for a beautiful woman."

"Sweet," I said, kissing him. "Is this you, apologizing?"

"Yes." He nodded. "I've been a prick. About Christmas. And family. And everything."

"You have been pretty awful," I agreed.

He wrapped his arms around my waist. "I'm going to do better. I swear it, Weezie."

"I know," I said, kissing him.

"No, really," he said. "You make everybody around you happy. You make me happy. I don't tell you that enough, but you do."

"That's quite a speech," I said, nuzzling his neck. "Is that my Christmas present? Because if it is, it's a really good one. I've got a good present for you too. Wanna see?"

"I'm not done yet," he said carefully. "I've been thinking about this all night. Even before Paula—I mean, my mother—

showed up. I'm tired of blaming other people for the way my life turned out. Because it didn't turn out so bad, you know?"

"I know."

"I've got a home, and a great business. A family—even though they drive me nuts, I've got a family. And I've got you. I can't imagine what my life would be like without you."

"Even though I drive you nuts?"

"Especially because you drive me nuts. I get to choose—whether to be happy or miserable. I choose happy. I choose you, Weezie Foley."

He kissed me, long and slowly and thoroughly.

"I choose you back," I said when I came up for air.

Without warning, he sank down into the big leather arm-chair by the fireplace and pulled me onto his lap.

"Is this the part where you ask me if I've been a good little girl this year?" I asked, giggling and fumbling with his belt buckle.

"We'll get to that part," he said, kissing me hungrily and running his hands up under my sweater. "Although, to be honest, I have to say I prefer you naughty. Actually, I was thinking we'd do the present part now."

"I do *love* presents," I said, working on his shirt buttons.

"We'd better do the presents first," he said, pushing me upright. "Or we might not get around to it tonight."

"Me first," I said.

Fortunately, Manny and Cookie's redecorating scheme had left Daniel's little pile of presents at the front edge of the tree. I gathered them into my arms.

"All that for me?" he said, his face falling. "I only got you one."

"Only one of these is really special," I assured him. "The others are nothing. They can wait till tomorrow."

I climbed back onto his lap, carrying only the tall, cylindrical gift that I'd wrapped in heavy gold paper with a thick blue velvet ribbon. "Open it," I commanded.

He untied the ribbon with a single tug and slipped the bottle out of the paper.

"Wow," he said, reading the label aloud. "A 1970 pomerol. My God, Weezie, this is an amazing bottle of wine. Where'd you find it?"

"An auction," I said anxiously. "You like it?"

"I will," he said, running his fingertips over the cork.

"It's a 1970," I said. "Because of the year you were born. I wanted to buy you a special bottle, and BeBe said this would be good."

"Better than good," he said. "Life-altering." He shifted, sliding out from under me and standing up. "Stay there. I'll be right back."

When he came back, he was carrying a corkscrew and two wineglasses. Before I could stop him, he'd plunged the opener into the cork.

"Wait!" I protested. "Daniel, this is a once-in-a-lifetime bottle. You don't know what I had to go through to buy it. I mean, I love that you're excited about it, but don't you want to save it for a special occasion?"

He poured a few drops into one of the glasses, rolled it around, then held it to his nostrils, inhaling deeply and smiling widely. He tasted, nodded, then poured a glass and handed it to me.

I sniffed dutifully. And sipped. It was very good wine, as far as I could tell. But then, I thought the screw-top stuff I bought at Kroger was good too.

Daniel sipped his, then carefully set his glass down on the coffee table.

My heart sank. "Not so hot, huh? I've got some champagne too, but maybe we'd better wait on that."

"Later," he said. "Now it's my turn." He scooted me over to one side and raised a hip to reach into his pocket.

He brought out a small black velvet box and held it out to me. "Sorry about the wrapping," he said. "I was going to wait until tomorrow. But you said I should save the wine for a special occasion. This is as special as it gets."

My hands were damp and shaky, and my fingers couldn't quite work the tiny silver clasp on the box.

"Here," he said impatiently. He took the box and flipped the top open.

A circlet of blue sapphires winked and sparkled in the reflected light of the Christmas tree, and in the center of the sapphires sat one perfect square-cut diamond.

"I know they're not your birthstones, but you love blue, and they're sapphires, and just a diamond didn't seem like enough—"

"Shut up," I said, kissing him quiet.

"Yes?" he asked, a little while later, taking the ring from the box and fitting it on my trembling left hand.

"Yes," I whispered. "Oh, *hell* yes."

acknowledgments

First and foremost, thanks go to Carolyn Marino, my amazing editor at HarperCollins, for the idea to set a Christmas novella in Savannah, and to Stuart Krichevsky, the best agent in the world, who convinced me I actually *could* write a story in less than four hundred pages. Thanks and hugs also go to Polly Powers Stramm and Jacky Blatner Yglesias, for their unfailing help and friendship, and to food writer and cookbook author extraordinaire Martha Giddens Nesbit, for her encyclopedic knowledge of Savannah foodways—and the inspiration for our family's favorite crab cakes. Ed Herring at Seaboard Wine Warehouse in Raleigh helped with wine research, and Liz Demos, owner of my favorite antiques shop in Savannah, @Home Vintage General, showed me how Weezie's shop should be run. David K. Secrest helped with sports info, and friends like Virginia Reeve and Ron and Leuveda Garner gave me shelter on Tybee Island. And as always, thanks and love to my family, Hogans and Trochecks, and now Abels, whose love remains the best Christmas gift of all.

MARY KAY ANDREWS is the *New York Times* bestselling author of *The Beach House Cookbook* and more than thirty novels, including *Bright Lights, Big Christmas, The Homewreckers, The Santa Suit, The Newcomer,* and *Hello, Summer.* A former journalist for the *Atlanta Journal-Constitution,* she lives in Atlanta, Georgia.

www.marykayandrews.com

FOLEY FAMILY IRISH CORNED BEEF DIP

The way you class up a recipe calling for canned corned beef is to serve it in a hollowed-out bread round bought at the best bakery in your neighborhood. Preferably the bread should be rye, pumpernickel, or sourdough.

1 ⅓ cups sour cream

1 ½ cups Duke's mayonnaise

2 teaspoons dried minced onion

1 12-oz. can corned beef

½ teaspoon jarred horseradish cream

2 round loaves unsliced bread

Combine all ingredients except the bread, mashing with a fork to create even consistency. Spoon into one hollowed-out bread round. Serve with cut-up chunks of the second loaf of bread.

DROP COOKIES

s all-purpose flour

poon baking soda

spoon salt

p softened butter

up powdered sugar

cup granulated sugar

cup vegetable oil

large eggs

2 teaspoons almond extract

FROSTING:

½ cup softened butter

½ teaspoon almond extract

½ teaspoon vanilla extract

2½–3½ cups powdered sugar

3 tablespoons milk (any kind)

Food coloring of your choice

Preheat oven to 350 degrees.

In large mixing bowl combine the first three dry ingredients. Cream butter into flour mixture. Add both kinds of sugar and beat until fluffy. Add oil, eggs, and almond extract to mixture and beat until well mixed.

Chill cookie dough in refrigerator for 30 minutes.

Pinch off teaspoon-sized bits of dough, roll between fingertips, and place on ungreased cookie sheet, a half inch apart. After all cookies are on sheet, use back of a teaspoon to flatten cookie and make impression on top.

Bake 10–12 minutes, until cookies are palest shade of yellow. Makes about five dozen cookies.

Make frosting: Beat butter into powdered sugar, then add almond and vanilla flavorings. Thin with milk until you have a thick frosting, separate into two or more bowls, and tint with desired shades of food coloring. Red and green are fun for Christmas. Place a dab of frosting atop each cookie.

These keep well in a sealed container.

RED ROOSTERS

A Christmassy cocktail that will make your gues.
remember to make it the night before your party so th
to freeze. And remind guests that this potable is migh
makes ten servings. As if!

¼ cup granulated sugar

½ cup water

1 cup frozen lemonade
concentrate

1 cup frozen orang
concentrate

2 cups cranberry juice

2 cups vodka

4 cups ginger ale

Bring sugar and water to a boil in a large saucepan over
heat, stirring until sugar dissolves. Add all juices and voc
and stir to blend. Freeze mixture in a freezer-safe pitcher
other container. One hour before serving, add ginger ale (or
transfer mixture to a pitcher, then add ginger ale). As mixture
thaws, break into slush with a long spoon.

FAIRY

4½ cu

1 teas

1 tea

1 cu

1 c

½

1

2

REDNECK CAVIAR

This dip is healthy, colorful, and addictive. Serve with thicker corn chips, or scoop up with celery sticks or bell pepper triangles.

2 15.5-oz. cans black-eyed peas, drained and rinsed

1 10-oz. can diced tomatoes with green chilies, drained

1 small yellow bell pepper, finely diced

½ red bell pepper, finely diced

½ red onion, diced

½ cup pickled okra

½ cup fresh cilantro, chopped

½ cup olive oil

¼ cup apple cider vinegar

Combine the vegetables in a bowl and stir. In separate bowl whisk together oil and vinegar, then stir into the black-eyed-pea mixture.